29 р.

G000153848

PETER PAN
AND THE
ONLY CHILDREN

By the same author
ALICE THROUGH THE NEEDLE'S EYE

"Bee came swimming towards them."

PETER PAN
AND THE
ONLY
CHILDREN

GILBERT ADAIR

WITH EIGHTEEN ILLUSTRATIONS
INCLUDING NINE COLOUR PLATES
BY
JENNY THORNE

E. P. Dutton / New York

To Ralph
this book is, as I am,
dedicated

First published in the United States in 1988 by
E. P. Dutton, a division of NAL Penguin Inc.,
2 Park Avenue, New York, N.Y. 10016.

Originally published in Great Britain by
Macmillan Children's Books.

Library of Congress Cataloging-in-Publication Data
Adair, Gilbert.
Peter Pan and the only children.
Summary: Ten-year-old Miranda mysteriously jumps from
the ship carrying her and her family from India to
England and meets Peter Pan, who now resides beneath the
waters of the Indian Ocean.
[1. Fantasy] I. Thorne, Jenny, ill. II. Title.
PR6051.D287P4   1987   823'.914 [Fic]   87-13653

ISBN: 0-525-24616-9

OBE

1 3 5 7 9 10 8 6 4 2

First American Edition

CONTENTS

COLOUR PLATES

CHAPTER I
Overboard!

No man is an island. An English poet once made that statement, which seemed so profound it was thereafter held to be true always. He meant that no man stands alone, that each man has need of all his fellow human beings. But every rule, like almost every family, has its black sheep. In a family this might be the uncle whose name is always spoken in whispers or the second cousin who, when last heard from, was tea-planting in the East Indies: where a rule is concerned we call it an exception. And the hero of this story, in fact like the heroes of most good stories, is just such an exception. He *is* an island, far from all the regular shipping lanes. Like every island he despises the mainland and the only company he is willing to put up with is that of other islands like himself. (He sneers at the half-breed peninsula.) Yet like them, too, his most secret longing, so secret he will never admit it even to himself, is that one day the treasure buried within him will be discovered. Let's you and I go hunt that treasure.

Our tale properly begins aboard a passenger steamer somewhere in the middle of the Indian Ocean, on one of those shipping lanes that islands shun. The world, you know, is not unlike a Christmas pudding except that, if you think of the Arctic and the Antarctic Circles, it has been adorned with a scoop of brandy butter on both top and bottom; and the Indian Ocean is the expanse of high sea that stretches between the triangular sub-continent of India and the brandy butter of the Antarctic Circle. I ought, I suppose, to give you the ship's exact position, but by the time I had its latitude and longitude all worked out, it would have steamed a few knots further on and I should have to start all over again. Enough to know that in whichever direction we peer it is as if there never had existed such a thing as land.

Of course the ship we speak of was creamy white in colour and it had three slanting white funnels with red tips; and the sight of its elegant passengers strolling uncaringly along its upper decks or playing quoits and shuffleboard quite made you forget the grimy engines chugging away in its depths and the red-hot furnaces which were tended day and night by stokers whose brawny tattooed bodies glistened with sweat. It belonged to the P & O (Peninsular & Oriental) Line and was bound for England from the colonies.

The third and fourth cabins on 'C' Deck, on the left side of the passageway looking towards the Gulf of Aden, were occupied by a Major Porter of the Indian Army, Mrs. Porter and their daughter Miranda.

Major Porter was pretty much in charge of a small island off the southern tip of India. I won't bother you with the name of the island, which was so insignificant not even its own inhabitants had ever heard of it; but the Major referred to himself as a big fish in a little pond and he presided over it with an hauteur that would not have shamed the Viceroy himself, whose hand he had shaken on one unforgettable occasion. Ruddy-faced, tall and erect, he would have looked every inch the Empire-builder were it not for the fact that he lacked a most essential particular: a strong chin. Inwardly he did not feel chinless, quite the reverse; and in the performance of his duties he did everything in his power short of standing on his head to distract His Majesty's farthest-flung subjects from a chin that was not there. Chinless he undoubtedly was, however, and although his father had been chinless, and his father before him, and although there hung in the ancestral Porter home a portrait of his great-grandfather whose unique *double*-chinlessness the artist had captured with uncanny and uncalled-for realism, our poor Major could not rid himself of the suspicion that it was that which had denied him the promotion he rightly deserved.

At these moments Mrs. Porter hastened to reassure him. "But, my dear," she would say, "the Colonel's wife told me only the day before yesterday that you were first in line for promotion, and she made no mention of your chin."

"How could she," he would reply bitterly, "when I have next to no chin to mention? Oh, it is too unjust!"

Or, after he had returned in a huff from an evening at his Club: "I am sure nothing personal was intended, Henry. It is quite a normal thing to say 'Chin-chin' when raising one's glass."

But he would not be consoled. It was the tragedy of his life. And when I think of the infinitely more dreadful tragedy that is about to overwhelm him, I feel the unfairness of it almost as if I were in his place. He will need all the strength and steadfastness he possesses in the dark days ahead. Suppose, then, we give him or rather lend him a chin, a real chin, to help him bear up manfully through the coming ordeal. Just for the duration of the adventure, mind you – suppose we add a chin while he is not looking, the way children will scribble moustaches on to the more tempting faces on advertising hoardings.

Yes, let's.

There, that is much better. He is now the man he has always felt himself to be, able to face both the world and the shaving-mirror – at 7.30 a.m. it is much the same thing – without flinching.

Already he has started to bustle about the cabin with a brand new sense of purpose. England! They were going to England!

It's true that he enjoyed being a Major in the Indian Army and he did not even mind being a big fish in a little pond. But the Porters had been on their island for two whole years without so much as a glimpse of home and he was itching to breathe in the soft evening air on the Downs. And if Phileas Fogg, the hero of Jules Verne's book *Twenty Thousand Leagues Under the Sea*, played Patience while crossing the Atlantic, the Major played Impatience, in a manner of speaking. He would have exchanged every quoit on the P & O Line for a good grassy game of bowls. He visited the ship's engine-room and inspected the stokers' tattoos with the air of somebody whose mind is on green hedgerows. If ever he had an idle moment he would anxiously scan the horizon as if the other extremity of the Indian Ocean lapped up against the White Cliffs of Dover. And now he had a real chin to stroke as he rapturously day-dreamed about cricket stumps and brown ale and—

"Henry! Henry dear, it's nearly dinner-time!"

It was Mrs. Porter, the Major's 'darling Lillibet'. She

was a lovely one with fair hair which curled over her shoulders when it was unpinned at night and eyelashes you would willingly have laid down your life for. And when the Major entered the adjoining cabin she did not notice the sudden change in him for the simple reason that in her eyes he had always had a fine, strong, manly chin.

"Say goodnight to Miranda, dear. But quickly, we mustn't keep the Captain waiting."

In fact, they did not actually dine at the Captain's table, but *near* it, as the Major liked to say; but if she suspected that he was in one of his low, chinless, unpromoted moods, Mrs. Porter was perfectly content to go along with the pretence that the whole first-class dining-room would be incommoded by a delay on their part.

On this occasion, fortunately, the Major did not need to be indulged. "Pooh!" he barked, jutting his chin quite as to the manner born. "We are not schoolchildren to be summoned to table on the very stroke of the hour. Besides, I wish to give my favourite daughter a kiss."

Now, since a woman's age is sometimes a delicate business, let's just say that if you asked Miranda how old she was on practically any day other than her birthday itself she was still young enough to answer "something-*and-a-half*". Yet she was also old enough to have made the discovery that a particular way she had of extricating a wisp of hair from her cheek could be not merely practical but rather charming. She was, in a word, ten.

Was she excited to be going home? Well, the word 'home' had a special meaning for her, exactly the contrary of what it signifies for the rest of us. Home was somewhere far, far away, on the other side of a line called the Equator, to which you travelled by steamship. Every time you got there you seemed to be a different size since everybody you were presented to would exclaim "My, how she's grown!" It was inhabited by funny-smelling people who would sit you on their laps and say "You don't remember me but I remember you", when you remembered them all without fail. It was a place with neither monkeys nor monkey-puzzle trees, where you were expected to remain on your best behaviour for days on end and where you had nothing to do and nobody to talk to – no younger brothers and sisters (they were all younger than she and they were all left behind) to cuddle or scold, no Timothy or Firouz or Anahita or, the littlest of them all as well as the naughtiest, Ben. (If some of these names sound unusual ones for an English family, I shall explain more fully in the next chapter.)

"Now, my dear child," said her father, bending over the bunk, "and are we ready for sleep?"

"Yes, father."

"No silly dreams tonight, I trust?"

"But, father, I can't help them coming."

Miranda knew herself too well to promise her father that she would not dream her silly dreams. It happened every night, and at ten one is too old a dog to be taught new tricks.

"After all, nobody can help dreaming, Henry dear," sighed Mrs. Porter, with the sweet reasonableness of someone who knows whereof she speaks.

"If I have said it once, I have said it a hundred times," the Major replied, and he had, he had, "it's not the

6

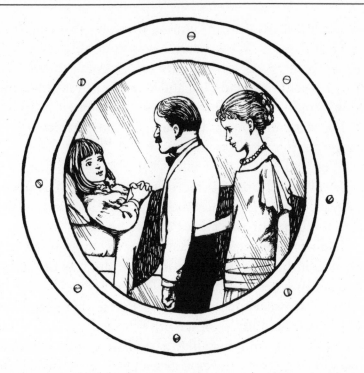

dreaming I object to but the dreams. I will not have my daughter – ten years old, my dear, a mere ten years old! – consorting with people to whom you and I have never been introduced, and such a riffraff set they sound, too. I wouldn't have her meet them by day, so my resolve is all the stronger that she decline any invitations for the dead of night."

"But, father," said Miranda, who could twist the Major round her little finger, especially when that little finger was twisted round a stray wisp of hair, "I cannot choose the people I meet in my dreams."

But he wouldn't relent. "And why not, I would like to know? Why not? One chooses the books one reads, does one not? One chooses the plays one goes to see.

Ergo, you must learn to choose the company you keep in your dreams. Why, when I was your age, my girl, I would have to tell my parents before going to bed just how I meant to spend each and every one of my sleeping hours, and it was all the worse for me the next morning if I'd wandered from the straight-and-narrow. It's a simple matter of disciplining yourself."

"Yes, father."

"And you'll promise me to try to dream of real and pleasant things, like hollyhocks and skylarks and brown ale – well, not brown ale, of course, but—"

"I do promise to *try*," said Miranda, though she had no notion how to go about it, since she was of course fast asleep when the dreams stole over her.

But that was enough for Major Porter. He kissed her gently on the middle of her brow, exactly as you snuff out a candle; and just like a snuffed candle Miranda instantly closed her eyes and snuggled deep inside her bed. The Major and his Lillibet then softly tiptoed across the polished cabin floor and with one last, departing glance at their offspring switched off the little night-light and went to dine.

Thus the night-light had been switched off. *But the moon had been left switched on.* This, you must realise, was due to no lack of foresight on the part of the Major and his good wife. There was nothing either they or anybody else could do about a bright, full tropical moon suspended in the night sky. Yet perhaps half the troubles besetting the world might vanish away if only we were able to switch off the moon. Perhaps, if they had not been infected by its crazy humours, husbands and wives would stop having the terrible quarrels that they some-

"There came walking along the deck an elderly,
dinner-suited gentleman."

times do and statesmen would not so recklessly wage wars nor murderers so zealously stalk their victims. Unfortunately the moon is a fact, which is to say, it's an opinion of God; although He has been known to change His mind on occasion, He has never yet seen fit to prevent the moon from rising at its due hour to its appointed rank in the heavens.

On this particular night the moon – which, as I say, was full and bright – shone directly through the cabin port-hole, casting an eerie halo of light over Miranda's head. The child frowned in her sleep without knowing the reason why. She drowsily moaned once or twice and shifted uncomfortably, though her mattress could not have been more feathery. Then her eyes sprang open wide, like a pair of tiny suitcases that had been packed too tight. What was that she heard?

In the darkness Miranda did not understand how she knew that somebody or something had addressed her, she just knew it. So she listened with rapt attention now, in the hope that the voice might speak again.

It did. And what it most distinctly said was, of all unlikely things, "It's a braw, bricht, moonlicht nicht the nicht."

It's a braw, bricht, moonlicht nicht the nicht?

To tell the truth, it was the voice itself, not anything it had to say, that puzzled her; a voice so strangely disembodied it was hard to credit that it had emerged from a mouth and that the mouth belonged on a face and that the face was attached to a body. Once more it whispered, "It's a braw, bricht, moonlicht nicht the nicht." And this time, for she was now as wide awake as could be, Miranda was certain it had come from just outside the cabin door. In an instant she had slithered out of her little upper berth, dropped to the ground and, still in her night-gown, made her way to the door. But when she opened it nobody at all was standing there. The passageway was deserted.

"It's a braw, bricht, moonlicht nicht the nicht."

Now it came from further off, sounding like a siren with a Scots accent. It seemed to Miranda that, if speaker there were, he must be concealed just around the corner, where the passageway connected up with the main channel on 'C' Deck. When she arrived there, however, no one was to be seen and the mysterious voice began teasing her from the top of the stairs leading to the deck itself. And if in her whole extraordinary adventure there was a point at which the Inevitable locked itself in and slipped the bolt, it was doubtless the moment when Miranda fearlessly climbed the stairs and found herself alone on deck. For from that moment on there could be no turning back.

The moon was high. The very lightest of breezes turned the pages of the sea. From the steamship's first-class dining-room could be heard the busy to-ing and fro-ing of waiters, the rumour of civilised table-talk and the soft, euphonious clatter of silver cutlery. Yet rising above, or else cutting through, these sounds was a faint rustle of a voice that emanated from the depths of the ocean itself: "It's a braw, bricht, moonlicht nicht the nicht."

The whole world seemed to be holding its breath. But just as the child stepped over to the rail and peered into the sea there came walking along the deck an elderly, dinner-suited gentleman with twinkling eyes and a drooping moustache. He was a Scot, so it was said, an author of no inconsiderable fame and the cynosure of the Captain's table. As he later described the scene, in a manner so enthralling that many of his listeners felt prompted to enquire of the purser what books of his they might obtain, he saw what appeared to be a little girl in her night-gown ease herself through the bars of the rail, then, before it quite dawned on him what was happening, hold her nose and plunge over the side.

When he had regained his composure, he rushed to the spot.

Too late! Miranda – "ten years old, my dear, a mere ten years old!" – was already encircled by a score of evil black fins (which, in these waters, has ever meant only one thing). The fins converged inexorably on their helpless, flailing prey until, with a frightful scream followed by a detestable whooshing noise as of a plug being drawn out of a bathtub, both they and she disappeared beneath the surface of the ocean.

CHAPTER II

"We Two are Orphans Now"

The alarm went up at once and the Captain switched the engines off. A lifeboat was lowered, whose crew rowed back and forth, back and forth, calling "Mir-a-anda! Mir-a-anda!" into the night, quite the most desolate sound you could ever think to hear. However, it was all in vain, indeed just a formality, for when the last tiny bubble of air had burst on the surface the last hope for the child had gone, and the only possible outcome was that which was now in every passenger's mind but of which no one dared speak in so many words.

And what, you ask, of Major Porter and his wife?

He received the news with a face so ashy-white that had I not lent him a new chin I think he might well have leapt into the ocean himself. As for Mrs. Porter, she fainted away, and on the orders of the ship's doctor was immediately transported to her cabin. There for the longest time she lay caught in the net of Death's lengthening shadow, until at last she freed herself from it by the strength of her soul. Her soul, you understand, not her heart; for that fragile organism had not merely been broken but shattered beyond repair, and if she went on living, and patiently submitted to the duties and responsibilities that come with each passing day, I can only say that there are far more people than you would ever suspect who are at present walking about with broken hearts, like those rugger players who discover only when the match is ended that they have fractured a rib or two.

They would sit there in the cabin, just a few hours after the dreadful event, recollecting Miranda and her ways in so intense a fashion that even though their eyes brimmed with tears the child appeared more vividly in front of them than if she had been alive still.

"Her smile, Henry. Oh, her smile," cried Mrs. Porter, "that she took after you."

"I will never smile again," said the Major, as if it were one promise he intended to keep.

"And her eyes! Why did we not appreciate her eyes when we could?"

"We did, my love."

"And that lovely way she had of coiling a wisp of hair around her pinkie when it fell on her brow."

"Oh, don't, don't!"

That last memory was simply too much for the Major. His upper lip retained a proper military-style stiffness, but the lower one started to wobble alarmingly, and if he had held off a second longer he would most likely not have been capable of speaking at all.

"We must be brave, my darling Lillibet, awfully brave. We must remember that Miranda is in Heaven now where no harm can reach her."

"Heaven?" Mrs. Porter repeated in a wondering tone, almost as if she had just come to hear of the place. "But she has never been away from home by herself before. She will be dreadfully homesick, I know. Oh, how foolishly I'm speaking!"

"No, that is not foolishness," said her husband

gravely, "for I can well believe that one might feel a little homesick there at the beginning."

"But what will become of us, my dear? We two are orphans now."

The sight of the little upper berth, unoccupied, its blankets tossed back so untidily it momentarily deluded them into believing that Miranda was being as naughty as she had been on many a former occasion, and had to be scolded for it, would have made Mrs. Porter break down altogether had they not been interrupted by a discreet knocking at the door.

It was the Captain, who had not spoken to the unhappy parents since the moment the alarm was first raised. He stood before them, shifting his peaked cap nervously from one hand to the other like a piece of hot toast.

"My dear Mrs. Porter – Major – forgive the intrusion, but I wished to see if there was something I might do for you. What a terrible, terrible thing to have occurred. I am keenly aware of my own share of the responsibility, but how could one know, how could one know?"

"There is no burden of responsibility that you have to bear," said the Major; "none whatsoever."

"Oh, but there is," the Captain insisted, "except that in this case the circumstances were so very different, you see, that I didn't think—"

"Why, what circumstances do you mean?" asked Mrs. Porter.

The Captain began haltingly. "It is said – I won't say that it is true, you understand, only that it is said – in this part of the Indian Ocean on moonlit nights – it always happens on moonlit nights – a number of small children have been persuaded by some unseen force or influence to disappear over the side of a ship – just such a ship as this."

His listeners were spellbound.

"A mere legend, you will say, as I once did," the Captain went on, "yet cases have been recorded with a disturbing frequency."

"And you say that it happens only to children?" enquired the Major.

"Not exactly," the Captain replied; "and that's the strangest part of all. It happens to *only* children."

The Major and his wife looked at each other aghast.

"To only children, yes," he continued; "which is why I didn't feel any need to tell you. Pooh-pooh it as you no doubt will, as any sensible person would, I consider it nevertheless my duty to warn all parents on board with an only child of such occurrences – a light-hearted warning, you know, as a story that should be taken only half-seriously, but a warning all the same. But since Miranda – ah me, what a charming little thing she was, but with a hint of sadness about her, too – since she had so often spoken to me of her brothers and sisters, how she would play mother to them, scolding them then cuddling them, why, I didn't think there was any reason on earth to bring up the silly tale at all."

At this new information Mrs. Porter dissolved in tears.

The temperature of the Captain's peaked cap, which had cooled down meanwhile, once again seemed to be rising, since it obviously pained him to hold it in either hand for more than a split second.

"My dear lady, I – I fail to understand."

"Miranda *was* an only child!" groaned Mrs. Porter, burying her face in her hands.

"An only child? Bless my soul," said the Captain, "I was led to believe – Miranda made particular mention of her little brother Ben and what a scamp he could be at times."

"Imagination, sir, imagination," interposed Major Porter, who saw it all now. "A lonely child's imagination, no more than that."

The story had to be told. How Miranda from an early age had been a dreamer, and what she loved dreaming about more than anything was that she had lots of brothers and sisters, whom she would christen after the few children she knew and who in her mind partly resembled those children and were partly figments of her imagination, as is the way with dreams. Thus *her* Ben, just like the Ben who was the youngest son of the island's Customs and Excise Officer, was flaxen-haired and had a fondness for making his cheeks go pop by inserting his index finger inside his mouth then quickly drawing it out again: that apart, there was no resemblance between them. And *her* Timothy could certainly have held his own in any stand-up scrape against his namesake, Timothy Brown, whose father was the Major's adjutant: on the other hand, the imaginary Timothy got much the better school marks of the two. As for Firouz and Anahita, they were, as you may have guessed by now, the names of two children belonging to Miranda's Indian nurse – her *amah*, as such nurses are called – and they, too, soon became part of her dream-family.

Other little girls play with dolls, of course, and

sometimes half-imagine they are real people. But when they talk to them and spank them for misbehaving, you have got to see that from a grown-up's point of view it is reassuring to know that they are at least talking to something – to a thing if not to a real person. What the Porters found so perplexing was to see their daughter chattering away to no one or nothing at all, and telling bedtime stories as if a whole brood of infants were hanging on every word (so convincingly on occasion that Mrs. Porter had to look twice to make quite certain Miranda was alone). She had been chided for it, but to no avail; and, as we have seen, most upsetting to the Major were her night-dreams, when she and the children in her charge would all regularly uncover some nest of rebels in the hills or be kidnapped and held to a fabulous ransom – even if, thank goodness, everything would come right as a rule by morning.

So there it was, Miranda's whole sad story. When the Captain had listened to it, he shook his head in a woebegone fashion. "If I had only known," he sighed, "perhaps this terrible tragedy might have been averted."

"You have no reason to blame yourself, Captain," was what the Major replied. "It is a cruel joke that Fate has played on us."

On which enigmatic observation the Captain again offered his condolences and took his leave of them.

We shall follow his example, for the present at least. It might, though, be worth mentioning one further incident which took place on board that unfortunate ship. You will not be surprised to learn that Miranda's fatal plunge cast a pall over the remainder of the long ocean voyage. The combined enchantments of an equatorial

moon and the watery blue quilt of the sea seemed vastly
diminished when one remembered that the moon had
been party to a child's unnatural and untimely death,
and that somewhere beneath the silken crest of moon-
light playing over the sea there lurked shoals of evil
black fins just waiting to – then one shuddered and
hurriedly changed the subject of conversation.

The Major and his wife kept a great deal of the time to
their cabin; when they did venture forth they were
greeted by the terrifying politeness that always accom-
panies a bereavement. But one evening, about a week
later, they were taking the air on deck together when
they found themselves accosted by the literary gentleman who had witnessed Miranda's disappearance. He
had come strolling from the opposite direction, placidly
smoking a cigarette, but when he saw them approach he
stepped forward and greeted them.

"Let us dispense with introductions," he said to the
startled couple. "You know who I am and I know who
you are, and I shouldn't for the world invade your
privacy if I didn't believe I could give you a message of
hope."

Mrs. Porter flushed. "Hope?" she echoed uncertainly.
"Hope . . . for Miranda?"

"Steady there, my love," said the Major under his
breath, and if a beetle-browed frown could kill, the
stranger would have dropped like a stone.

"Yes, for Miranda," he bluntly continued, dodging
the Major's frown. "You see, Mrs. Porter, if there's one
race on earth I claim to understand, it's that of children.
When I was a boy myself and I was asked like a hundred
thousand boys before me what I wanted to be when I

grew up, my answer wasn't anything in the usual line. I didn't want to be a general or even an engine-driver. No, what *I* answered was: a child. Which made me, of course, an old man before my time, since a real child wouldn't know what a child is exactly, let alone want to become one. Yet it gave me an understanding of the thing I fancy few grown-ups possess. And this is what I have to say to you," he went on, becoming more and more animated. "Children die many times before their true death: they are scalped by redskins and made to walk the plank by pirates and held to ransom by native rebels. And it would be a tragedy, Mrs. Porter, a dreadful, needless tragedy if you were to mistake such a play-death for the real thing! There," he smiled, "now that I've had my say I needn't detain you any longer."

Whereupon, ending his speech as suddenly as he had begun it, he nodded briefly to Major Porter and his wife, then continued his stroll as before.

"Famous author he may be," snorted the Major, staring at the receding figure, "the man is obviously raving mad!"

But all Mrs. Porter said, in a voice that was quiet and still, was "I wonder . . ."

CHAPTER III
The Descent

I would like you now, Reader, to cast your mind back to the moment when Miranda stood on deck and peered into the ocean. What did she see down there that caused her to dive in? Could she already make out the ring of fins? Above all, why, why, why did she jump?

The answers to these questions, if you wish to know, are: (1) Nothing; (2) No; and (3) Because she wasn't quite herself. I would not like you to think she was sleepwalking, because, from the moment she arose from her bunk to the moment she plunged in, Miranda was perfectly aware of what she was doing and where she was going. But whether it was the charm of that intriguing voice and the fact that it never stayed put but always turned up a little further on from where she was, or whether it was merely the effect of the full moon, the truth is, she quite forgot that nicely brought-up little girls do not leave their beds in the middle of the night and wander along the decks of a ship; and do not, most particularly, leap fully-clothed into the Indian Ocean without so much as a by-your-leave.

What I will allow is that she might have been half-asleep-walking, so to speak, with one foot in wakefulness and the other in slumber, as if these two states were adjacent English counties and she was standing on the border astride them. Her eyes were not entirely open and not entirely closed: they were *ajar*. And her ears wickedly sifted out all the safe sounds that were struggling to make themselves heard – I mean the sounds of waiters and diners and the tinkly dance-music played by the little string orchestra – so that they could hear the more distinctly that whispered refrain of "It's a braw, bricht, moonlicht nicht the nicht." In the state she was in, stepping off the side of a ship into the sea must have seemed almost as natural as stepping off the kerb of a pavement on to a busy street. As a matter of fact, just as she would have done had it merely been the street, before she jumped Miranda dutifully looked right, then left, then right again, to make certain not to land on some flying fish, for instance, or on a school of porpoises.

So there she was, alone in the Indian Ocean and (although she did not know it yet) surrounded by sharks. Certainly, the outlook could have been brighter. But before she had time to take in what was happening to her, she went under – with a sound that I can only describe as blub-blub-blub-glub-glub-glubble-blubble-bubble-whooooooh!

To start with, she felt as if she were inside a monstrous vat of jelly, twisting this way and that in its heavy gooseberry-green transparency. The surface of the ocean closed over her head like a lid, and in a frenzy she strove to open it up again; as she did so she became gradually aware that something else was moving around her, that there were other creatures besides herself inside the jelly-vat.

However she did not have any time to make out who or what they were, for the lid suddenly opened and let

her rise spluttering to the surface. There was the moon exactly where she had last seen it. There, too, gaily illuminated and appearing to list slightly, the ship's side towered over her; and in the few seconds left to her before she sank into the jelly again she just managed to glimpse, high above her head, leaning over the rail and frantically waving to her, a tiny figure with a drooping moustache and an expression of utter horror on his face. Then it was, for a second time, blub-blub-blub-glub-glub-glubble-blubble-bubble-whoooooh!

They say that when one is drowning the whole of one's life passes in review before one's eyes, but what is not so well known is that it unwinds in the opposite direction. The reason for this is that we are already dead in a way before we are born since we have not yet come into existence. Thus, when it *is* our turn to be born, Death, knowing it is going to reclaim us one day, does not release us into the world 'with no strings attached'. Instead, it keeps a hold on us by a kind of invisible leash made out of something very like elastic. At the beginning, when we are mere babes or children or even in the first flower of youth, the elastic hangs completely slack so that we may walk and run and play without any impediment. Later, when we grow middle-aged and start to complain about the creaking of our bones, what the doctors call arthritis is actually due to the elastic being stretched tighter and tighter the further we move away from our death-before-birth. Later still, when we grow really old, some of us are incapable of walking at all, so tight has the elastic become, and those of us who can usually need a cane or a pair of crutches to assist us. Finally, when Death has come to the decision that our allotted span of life has run its course, it gives one last pull on the elastic – if we are aged or infirm a short sharp tug will usually do the trick, but if by chance we are still relatively youthful when Death decides to recall us, the tug has to be so much more violent – and this sends us reeling backwards to the same condition from which we first emerged. Which is why, during the instant that remains to a drowning man before the very end, he sees his entire life speeding past him in reverse.

That is what happened to Miranda, except that, since she was a mere ten years old, she did not have too far back to go. And just as she was reaching her earliest childhood memory, which was of sucking on a stalk of rhubarb in a mysterious trellised garden (it was in

England before the Major had been posted to his island), she found herself once more bobbing on the surface.

Her lungs were filled with sea water, which made her splutter and gasp in a way that was quite dreadful to behold. Despite that, however, she remembered that if she were to sink a third time she would never surface again. Death, you see, generally takes us the first time around but, for reasons best known to itself, if somebody should happen to be drowning it becomes a little more sportsmanlike and makes it the best out of three.

So Miranda straightway determined to stop floundering as helplessly as she had been doing up to then and tried to remember what she had learned at her swimming lessons. But again too late! As she was gathering her wits about her, she saw at last those evil fins bearing down upon her from every side.

She cried out, and then was gone. A sprinkling of air bubbles appeared on the surface like raindrops falling upwards from below, then they too were gone. The lid of the ocean had closed for good, and you might have thought Miranda Porter had never existed.

Yet how can that be? For if you count the number of pages still to be turned you will see that this is the beginning, not the end, of our story. And to understand why, we are going to have to follow Miranda under the sea. We are going to have to hold our own noses and plunge right in after her.

Are you ready?

BLUB-BLUB-BLUB-GLUB-GLUB-GLUBBLE-BLUBBLE-BUBBLE-WHOOOOOH!

What she (like you and me) expected to find there were of course the smooth bodies and flapping tails of

" 'Why of course, it's Peter Pan!' "

the sharks that surrounded her. But what she actually did see were lots of dangling legs and arms, her own size as nearly as she could make out. The legs were clothed in royal blues and livid purples and bright, translucent reds, while the arms or rather the hands were all holding canes with elegantly carved handles and projecting metal spikes that fanned out to – and then she understood! What she had taken to be sharks' fins was in reality the black ribbing of umbrellas – and good, solid umbrellas, too, the best that money can buy, those stocked exclusively by Jas. Smith & Sons, New Oxford Street, London (Estd 1830).

Confusedly, now, she heard voices all around her. Even if these sounded a little gurgly-gargly, she was able to make out everything that was said.

"I have her!" cried one.

"Careful, Tom-Tom, watch out for her feet," said another.

"She's awfully heavy – but quite pretty," added a third.

"Pretty? You think so?" a girlish voice remarked in a sulky gurgle. "Oh, if you like that type, I suppose."

"You never like any type, Bee. You're just jealous!"

"I'm not!"

"You are, too!"

"Aren't!"

"Are!"

"Stop quarrelling, you two, and take an arm each."

"She's tumbling upside-down again, Ralph."

"Well, turn her around, won't you. Gently, now."

"Hold her hair, Bee, don't pull it."

"I'm not!"

"You know you are, too!"

"Aren't!"

"Are!"

"Oh, put a sock in it or she'll drown!"

"Serve her right, she's pulling every way at once."

"Well, so did you at first."

"You had better give her artificial inspiration, Ralph, she's fading fast."

"Righty-ho. Steer clear, everyone."

And just when she thought she was about to burst, Miranda felt two strong young hands around her neck, then somebody's mouth brushing against hers as if to plant a kiss on it. But it was the strangest kiss she had ever received, for the boy (although she could not see him properly something told her it was a boy) blew such a gust of air down into her throat that even if she was still not quite sure whether she had drowned, she immediately felt much better for it and avidly began to take in her surroundings.

A galaxy of little eyes were blinking at her curiously out of the gloom. When she was able to make things out more clearly, she saw that swarming around her were about a dozen children. Each of them carried a grown-up's black umbrella and was clad in a multi-hued outfit woven, from the look of it, out of the leaves of rare undersea plants: these the more fashion-conscious had adorned with pretty shell brooches and neat rows of coral buttons. Most of the children were smiling at her agreeably enough, although one or two, she could not help remarking, were not; and she had soon recovered herself sufficiently to wonder just which of them had referred to her as heavy and which had tugged at her hair with a wholly unnecessary firmness.

However that would have to keep till later, as for the moment two of the bigger boys were gently lifting her up and sitting her down again inside the most capacious of the umbrellas, which, when upturned, did duty as a very comfortable little coach. Best of all, bound to the ribbing by two strings of what certainly seemed to be pearls, was a beautiful seahorse that looked as if it had been carved out of ivory.

"Your seahorse-and-carriage, ma'am," announced the boy whom the others addressed as Ralph; and though he was swimming at the time, of course, he contrived to bow low before her. Miranda bowed back, even gracefully waving the palm of her hand as she had once seen the King do.

So began her descent.

With never an awkward jolt the seahorse moved slowly forward into the depths of the ocean, drawing Miranda behind it. Meanwhile the other children, taking their cue from Ralph, installed themselves upright inside their own umbrellas and by using the handles as rudders formed a solemn escort on either side of the new arrival.

Down, down they drifted. For Miranda it was like visiting the Aquarium from the inside. All about her she could see fish as flat as leaves and fish as striped as zebras and fish as white and fluffy as cockatoos. There were weird thistly plants that reminded her of the loofah in the bathtub at home and insects that could have been mistaken for cinnamon sticks and coral reefs twisted into the most fantastical shapes you could ever imagine. Every so often one of the children would steer his umbrella alongside Miranda's to get a closer look at her; and whenever Ralph suspected that she needed more air, he too would approach and give her a fresh kiss. So what with one thing and another it was quite the most pleasant and exciting trip she had ever taken.

But where would it all end? That was the question going through Miranda's head when a little spark of light suddenly glimmered in the bottle-green darkness beneath her. Although there was a definite risk that she would topple the umbrella, and herself with it, she craned over to see what had caused it.

There on the ocean bed, astride a coral rock, his legs akimbo and his hands grimly on his hips, there another boy stood and stared up at her with a defiant expression on his lovely pale features. Even from so far away Miranda already sensed that he was not as other boys are. He had a lonely, masterful air about him that made him stand apart. He seemed, moreover, strangely familiar to her, and she racked her brains to discover where she had seen him before.

At last she remembered. For on one of her visits home her *amah* had taken her to Kensington Gardens, where, as you probably know, there has been erected a mossy little statue of 'the boy who would not grow up'. And she gave out a squeal of delighted recognition: "Why, of course, it's Peter Pan!"

Because Miranda had not yet learned how to speak underwater none of the other children could hear her exclamation, which floated upwards enclosed within the brackets of an air bubble. But you might like to know that when the bubble burst on the surface of the ocean, her voice rang out clear as a bell and was overheard by the crew of a Persian dhow that was passing that way. Unfortunately not one of them spoke a word of English, so nothing was done about it.

Alone of all the children, however, Peter – for it was indeed he – had taught himself to bubble-read. And when he heard his name mentioned, he could not help grinning with pride, and another scintilla of light flashed forth from his sharp little milk-teeth.

CHAPTER IV

Peter's Story

S oon the umbrella in which Miranda was sitting
alighted gently on the ocean bed, followed in such
swift succession by all the others that for a moment
you would have said it was raining umbrellas. In their
turn her attendants stepped on to Wet Land (as they
called it, to differentiate it from dry land), vigorously
shook out their brollies as if they had just come into the
house from a downpour, and stood in a row, awaiting
Peter's approbation.

That was exceeding slow in coming, though, as Peter
had already learned how useful it could be for a commander to let his underlings stew a while before passing
judgment; till the suspense became so intolerable that
one of the smallest children, who was so plump and
round and stripy he made Miranda think of a beach ball
she had at home, eventually burst out, "We brung
her, Peter! And we didn't spill her – not a single
drop!"

Peter glared at the offender and bared his flashing
teeth, although not in a grin this time. He then nimbly
leapt down from the coral on which he was standing and
looked intently at Miranda, who at that instant was so
nervous and fluttery, I can tell you, that the inside of her
tummy would have been of the utmost interest to a
butterfly-collector in search of rare and exotic speci-
mens. But all he did was ask, "What is your name?"

"Miranda Victoria Porter."

The three words rose up to the surface in three consecutive little air bubbles, and if you looked closely you might have seen Peter's eyes narrowing as he followed what she had said.

Then: "Mine is Peter Pan."

"I know," Miranda replied simply.

Peter, of course, had known all along that she knew, since it was seeing her exclaim his name in surprise that had made him grin in the first place. But though he had many admirable qualities, of which we shall hear a good deal presently, personal modesty was not one of them, and it pleased him so much to have a reputation that he tended to harp on about it.

"I am very famous, am I not?" he crowed.

Despite being a bit shocked by such cockiness, Miranda was going to tell him about his statue in Kensington Gardens, and also about the book in which she had read of his adventures, when she again began to feel rather faint. And she was slightly disappointed that neither Peter himself nor the boy named Ralph, who hovered at his side as an aide-de-camp should do, offered her the kiss she was expecting. Instead, Peter nonchalantly tore a leaf off a fuzzy yellow plant growing at his feet and bade her chew on it:

"Do, it will make you feel ever so much better."

Doing as he bade her, Miranda immediately breathed in and out more easily. And what with the excitement of the trip, and meeting Peter Pan, it was only now it truly came to her where she was.

"But wait," she said to Peter in a puzzled voice, "I ought to have drowned by now, and so ought you. All of you," she added, addressing the assembled children, though not one of them, as I say, was able to bubble-read.

"Oh, anybody can live under the sea when he knows how," Peter coolly replied. "But I invented it, you know, all by myself."

"But how is it done?" asked Miranda, who was starting to get the knack of speaking underwater. (The secret, if you should ever find yourself in such a situation, is to move your lips as little as possible, like a ventriloquist who makes his doll chatter on while he drinks a glass of water.)

"You can swim, can't you?" said Peter.

"Yes."

"Living underwater is just like swimming, only more so."

"How do you mean?"

"Nobody can swim before he's taught. Afterwards it seems easy, but before you know how, you struggle and splutter and you can't breathe, so of course you drown."

"But I haven't drowned," Miranda insisted, "and I should like to know why not."

"Oh well, when I first came here to live," Peter went on, "I had to keep swimming to the surface for air, which was a nuisance, particularly if I happened to be in mortal combat with a shark at the time."

"Are you often in mortal combat with sharks?"

"Most afternoons," said Peter diffidently. "Well, it was then I discovered that, by chewing on these plants, I didn't have to go up nearly so often."

Because Miranda had once read in an encyclopaedia

that plants give off air, or something very like air, Peter's answer seemed to her quite logical.

"Of course," he added, "when you dropped in there weren't any plants around for you to chew, so Ralph had to give you artificial inspiration."

"Don't you sometimes give artificial inspiration any-way – just to stay in practice, you know?" Miranda asked, with a little catch in her voice that you would not have noticed unless you had been specially listening for it.

"Never," sneered Peter. "We have far better things to do with our time than to keep thimbling each other."

Thimbling! Yet Miranda knew very well that what Peter really meant was kissing. His pitiful ignorance in this matter was in the book she had read about him and which came back to her now. How he had lived on an island called the Neverland, which was so far away that to reach it you took the second to the right, and straight on till morning. His life there had been an endless round of adventures with his lost boys, with mermaids and redskins, and most of all with that fiendish band of cut-throats who took orders from none other than Captain Jas. Hook himself. So she asked Peter about the Neverland and why he no longer lived there.

"Neverland?" he pondered, screwing up his button nose. "Why, I've never been to Neverland."

For one moment at least, before he went on to talk about something else, he was telling no lie. At that moment he really believed he had never set foot on the Neverland. The Neverland had become a memory, you see, a time as well as a place, and memories were what Peter hated most in the world. If they were disagreeable ones, they plunged him into a melancholia which might take him a whole week to snap out of; if, on the other hand, they were agreeable, they appeared to suggest that things had once been better than they were now, which made him even more difficult to live with.

And so, although Miranda eventually did hear the story of how and why he left the Neverland, almost none of it came from Peter's own lips. She pieced it together from what she was told by the other children, a process that took several weeks. But because I, as the author, may rearrange the story in any order I please, I think it would be preferable to let you have it all in one go.

If you remember, then, after having been trounced by Peter in the deadliest of all their sword-fights, Hook had been hurled from his foul brig, the *Jolly Roger*, into the ocean. Therein lurked the crocodile whose massive jaws were already watering at the prospect of completing a meal begun so long before. You can but imagine, if you wish, how it must have ripped through Hook's body as smoothly as though it were a nice buttery corn-on-the-cob. Yet it has to be said to the victim's everlasting credit that nothing so became his life as the brusque manner in which he left it. No deposed monarch ever laid his crownless head on the executioner's block with more innate dignity than Hook bowing to his unhappy fate. He was very much a cut-throat's cut-throat, and his breeding showed through in the end, as breeding always does.

But what of Peter? A strange thing happened to him then, though perhaps it was not so strange after all. With Hook dead and gone, half of his own life drained out of him, as if it had been a twin brother he had slain. For it is true that enemies, especially arch-enemies such as Hook and Peter had ever been to one another, are often closer than many a friend or acquaintance. Peter, in any event, no longer knew what to do with himself. After you have defeated in honest combat Captain Jas. Hook, the only man the Sea-Cook ever feared, you might as well take early retirement.

On top of which, he felt betrayed. Not, you understand, by Hook, who carried off his role to the end without undue bitterness. Oh, he may have cursed and blasphemed and bitten his hook to the quick with fury, he did not once murmur a complaint. No, it was by his own side that Peter felt dreadfully let down, by the lost boys to whom he had given the best months of his life and by Wendy who had become a mother to them all.

After Hook's demise and the extermination of the pirates, Peter and the others had taken flight for England and the house at No. 14 where Wendy's real parents lived and had long been grieving for her and her brothers John and Michael. And the Darling nursery had looked so cosy and warm, smelling of good soap and hand-carved toys, with faithful Nana in attendance, that the lost boys felt they had been found again and begged Wendy's mother to become theirs as well.

Thus it was that Peter returned to the Neverland alone, which was wholly to Tinker Bell's convenience. Tinker Bell was of course Peter's own special fairy, who had taken none too kindly to having a mother on the island. Now, save for an occasional visit by Wendy at spring-cleaning time, she had Peter all to herself; and being a somewhat middle-class sort of fairy, her ambition was to make him, in the terrible words, *settle down*. Had there been a stockbroker's office in the Neverland you may be sure Tink would have had Peter apprenticed to it, from 9 to 5.30 every weekday, Saturday mornings optional. She fussed over him. She nagged after him. She insisted that he stick a thermometer in his mouth if he so much as sniffled. When, having massacred a war-party of redskins, he wearily returned home to the house he had built for Wendy, instead of offering congratulations she screeched at him for not wiping his feet before he came in and getting her carpet all bloodstained again. The last straw was when he found her one evening knitting him a pair of fairy slippers. It was, he muttered darkly to himself, high time to take his leave.

So Peter slipped away by night, swimming from the island just as fast as his strong little legs could carry him. He did not fly, as he would have risked being followed by Tink – fairies, however, are as fearful of water as cats are. The better to conceal himself from her he swam beneath the surface of the sea, exposing only his lips to the air and using his shadow as a pair of flippers. It was then, I fancy (for there are details in his story which will most likely never be told), that he discovered how to live underwater; and having no need for his troublesome shadow on the ocean bed he ripped it off altogether. (Since the day Wendy had sewn it back on to the soles of his feet it had never felt entirely comfortable somehow and its hem was forever coming loose.)

Swimming hard, he arrived at last at an uninhabited region of the Indian Ocean and made his home there. But Peter would not have been Peter if he had not had subordinates around him to boss about and to rescue

from danger and also, perhaps, to keep him company –
although *that* he never admitted. Nevertheless he would
make certain this time he suffered no betrayal. Since, in
spite of the daily quota of perils he guaranteed them in
the Neverland, the perfidious lost boys secretly went on
yearning for the mothers and fathers, the sisters and
brothers they could only half-remember anyway, he
decided that he would choose his companions from
among children with none, or at least fewer, of these
advantages and who would therefore not for one moment regret their lonely nurseries. Which is how, in the
depths of the ocean, he founded what he appropriately
named The Brotherhood of Only Children. The name
was appropriate in that only children are, if you think
about it, all brothers and sisters to each other.

That was the story Miranda heard, piecemeal, first
from one child, then from another, and filling in the gaps
for herself. It had become part of the folklore of Wet
Land and I think it is fair to say that she was both
horrified and terribly fascinated by it. And one day
when she had come to know Peter better – but I am
jumping ahead a little here and, as in all the best stories,
everything should be told in the proper order.

CHAPTER V
The Home Beneath the Sea

L et's now return to where we broke off, to the
moment when Miranda was confronted by Peter
and the only children. She was still seated inside
her umbrella-carriage (or brolly-bus, as it was more
familiarly known), for she felt it would be impolite to
rise from it before being invited to. Luckily, while the
children stared at her quite shamelessly, some of them
even passing whispered comments to each other, Peter
remembered his manners sufficiently to offer her his
hand.

"Will you swim this way, please," he said to her with
a grown-up kind of pomposity that sat very queerly on
his unbroken voice. Then almost at once dropping these
assumed airs and graces that did not become him at all,
he childishly cried, "O Miranda, you must see the
house and everything!"

Before that, there were the presentations to be made.
In fact so many children had to be introduced to her at
once that she would be struggling to retain in her mind
the names of the first four or five when being presented
to the sixth would cause her to forget the first, the
seventh naturally made her forget the second, with the
eighth the third went clean out of her head, and so on.
So, to make it easier for you than it was for her, I pro-
pose to introduce just four of them properly and let you
yourself imagine what the others must have been like.

First then, after Peter himself of course, comes Ralph, whose importance in the Wet Land scheme of things can be measured by the fact that he is the only member of the Brotherhood, bar Peter, who continues to be addressed by the name his parents gave him. (Peter persuaded the other children that it would be more fun for them if they had nicknames, although the truth is that he hoped they would forget their second names all the more quickly if he changed their first.)

Now, as the world has its share of born leaders, so there exist born seconds-in-command, and Ralph was one of these. Second only to Peter himself, he was the best swimmer, the bravest shark-killer and the most skilful pearl-diver. He was always respectful of Peter and practically never questioned his orders; but although he would not dream of leading a mutiny, if ever a mutiny were to destroy the harmony of the Brotherhood (and little did any of them realise that on one dreadful, unforeseeable occasion it would), it could only be instigated by Ralph. None of the others boasted even a tenth of the pluck and authority such a desperate measure would entail.

Certainly not Tom-Tom, the next to be passed in review. He not only respected Peter but slavishly imitated his every move. He had been extremely young when taken into the Brotherhood, you see, and had not yet stopped copying the grown-ups around him. Tom-Tom would sometimes follow Peter so closely on his expeditions that you could easily have mistaken him for the shadow which Peter had ripped off. And this made for trouble if Peter were stealthily gliding through some reeds and suddenly doubled back, for he would immediately collide with Tom-Tom, who thus incurred his wrath more often than he might have done had he not been so clinging. No man is a hero to his valet, the proverb tells us, but poor Tom-Tom was a valet to his hero.

After Tom-Tom comes Second Helping, the plump little creature who reminded Miranda of her beach ball. If he was called Second Helping it was for not one but three reasons:

One, as you might expect, was because he was forever asking for a second helping and even secretly snacked on minnows between meals. (Snacking was expressly forbidden by Peter for the very good reason that he wanted everybody to be in tip-top condition.)

Two, because a few minutes before being born he had asked God if he might have a second helping of tummy; and God, Who had been in an unusually good mood that day, agreed.

Three, because when his mother and father saw him, so fat and round and greedy, they instantly made up their minds to refuse a second helping of children. So he had remained an only child, which he did not mind too much, since he would help himself at table to the shares of his brothers-and-sisters-who-might-have-been.

As for Bee, the last on our list, her name was short not for 'Beatrice' but for 'Be quiet!'. Silence was not her native tongue. She was a bossy one, right enough, for whom nothing was ever *comme il faut*. For instance, she would insist that the children give their hands a good wash before they sat down to supper, which was really quite absurd considering they were already at the bottom of the Indian Ocean. I cannot tell you how silly it

"Peter slipped away by night."

made them feel to be scrubbing their hands as if there were a wash-basin in front of them, especially as there could be no question of drying. And because she was excessively proud of her hair, which certainly was long and golden, she shirked most of the duties assigned to her and spent her time lazily swimming back and forth in such a fashion that her curls would smear themselves across her face to the greatest effect.

Until Miranda's arrival Bee had been the only little girl in the Brotherhood, and the way it came about was this. Originally it consisted of boys only, who enjoyed getting up dolphin races or playing rough-and-tumble games together in and out the coral reefs, games they suspected a sister would heartily disapprove of.

By mistake, of course, it was sometimes a girl who responded to their call. In which case, not unlike an angler tossing a puny catch back into the river, they would contemptuously cast her back above the surface and hold her propped up there until she could be rescued. Naturally, as soon as they had got their breath back, the three or four little girls to whom this had happened tried to tell their parents what had befallen them. But they were never believed, and the ship's doctor invariably put it down to shock and advised complete rest and calm with all the curtains drawn in the cabin.

Eventually, however, without any of the boys coming right out and saying what it could be, there rose an obscure feeling that something was missing from their life in Wet Land. It was Tom-Tom who first ventured to express the feeling out loud, while a few of the boys were mending fishing nets and Bubbles, a little Negro

boy who was so black of skin he used to be scolded by his mother for getting dirty whenever he messed about with her cooking flour, accompanied them with a soulful little lullaby on his harmonica.

Perhaps it was the lullaby conjuring up faded, dog-eared memories that he imagined had been tucked away in the bottom drawer of his mind and forgotten, or the fact that mending nets always seemed like woman's work, but Tom-Tom looked up momentarily from his labours and said in a dreamy voice, "I wonder what it would be like to have a sister."

The other menders greeted this remark with mocking laughter.

"It *is* a Brotherhood, you know," jeered one.

"Listen to the baby!" sneered another. "Baby wants a little sister!"

"He'll be wanting his mummy next," a third added with a laugh that I think he meant to sound scornful.

During these exchanges Peter himself had been seated a little way off, staring into watery space, so that it was unclear whether he had paid attention to what was being said. But since he had made no comment up to then, Bubbles turned to him and cried, in his thick American accent, "Hey, Peter, didya hear the idea Tom-Tom had?"

"I did," said Peter, to whom such an idea had never occurred before. "As a matter of fact I had been thinking just the same thing myself."

At the notion that he had the same idea as Peter, even if Peter naturally had had it first, Tom-Tom blushed from ear to ear. He only hoped that Peter was not offended by his having spoken out of turn.

But this unexpected about-face on Peter's part – for nobody could forget how he had been treated by Tinker Bell – caused the boys to lapse into an uneasy silence. Ralph alone dared to voice a lingering doubt.

"But, Peter," he said boldly, "I once knew somebody who had a sister. She was the most awful pest, always ordering him to do his homework and not to lie on the bed with his shoes on. A sister can spoil everything."

"Was she an older sister?"

"Yes."

"I thought so," Peter nodded sagely. "Older sisters are quite beastly. They're ugly and they tell you off and they treat you as if you were their servant. We shan't have one of those."

Of course Peter had never had a sister, older or younger, and everything he claimed to know about them came from the stories the members of the Brotherhood liked to tell each other of an evening. If the question had arisen he would have been just as rude about step-mothers who, according to the same stories, were as uniformly wicked as older sisters were ugly.

"Younger sisters are the thing," he declared. "They enjoy playing boys' games and they don't mind getting their knees scraped. A younger sister is what we need."

And since, in spite of the boys' rather forced mockery, Peter had only said aloud what they had been wishing in secret, every one of them ardently looked forward to the time when they would have a younger sister of their own.

Unfortunately their first attempt was not a complete success. To be sure, Bee was indeed a younger sister to most of the boys as far as her actual age was concerned. But because she had spent her tender years terrorising a whole nursery of dolls her temperament and her temper were those of one quite a bit older, and a long time passed before a bitterly resentful Peter was prepared to renew the experiment. Meanwhile poor Tom-Tom was naturally held to blame for the idea, Peter having conveniently forgotten how he stole it from him.

Miranda was their second try, and the general opinion so far was that she looked highly promising material. And, the presentations done, the moment finally came for her to inspect her new home. Peter took her hand in his and raised her out of the umbrella. She was at first

44

impeded by her night-gown, which billowed round her feet like a parachute, but she quickly found her sea-legs, so to speak, and swam off in his wake.

Wherever she turned the flora and fauna seemed so very lazy, lazy and languorous, gracefully swaying back and forth as to the tootling of a mysterious flute that could not be heard by human ears. Shoals of tiny fish would wriggle past so close to her that she was able to stretch out her arm and touch them; but if she actually tried to catch one she discovered it to be as slippery to grasp as a bar of soap in the bath. Crabs sidled across the ocean bed beneath her like little ballerinas on points and nameless wormy creatures would briefly pop their heads out of the sand before burrowing back into it out of sight.

The other children followed behind. Peter had disciplined them always to swim in a neatly symmetrical, fan-shaped formation, just like the fish whose domain they shared. As a result, there were never any traffic jams in Wet Land. It was a most entrancing thing to see some purple dragon fish, let's say, travelling in a direction at right-angles to that of the Brotherhood, the two symmetries adroitly and courteously criss-crossing each other with not the slightest confusion or collision.

After about ten minutes of this they abruptly turned a corner – yes, there are corners at the bottom of the sea just as there are on land, as well as steep inclines and crossroads and roundabouts and busy thoroughfares and slightly sinister back alleys you took care to avoid late at night – and there, in the distance, nestling on the side of what resembled a mountain with its lid removed, was unmistakably the home, the castle and the general headquarters of Peter Pan's Brotherhood of Only Children.

Why don't we swim on ahead to check that everything is shipshape for Miranda's inspection?

For it is of course a ship, a fine two-masted schooner which went down with all hands on Boxing Day 1897. (None of the children know this, but I looked it up.) Barnacled and rusty on the outside, its interior, as Miranda is about to discover, is an Ali Baba's Cavern, everything a home ought to be from a child's point of view but never is. It has lots of surprising little hatchways and cubby-holes, fo'c'sles and galleys, bulkheads and bollards (whatever *they* are), funnels in the shape of question-marks which offer wonderful concealment during games of hide-and-seek and flights of steps which seem to go up to nowhere and come back down again none the wiser. Oh, and there are rows of hammocks for sleeping in and engine-rooms for letting off steam in, and inside what must have been the main stateroom there hang official-looking portraits of solemn, bushybearded sea-captains whose eyes will so dart about because of the swelling of the ocean they look as though they are peering at your portrait instead of the other way round. These are used as dartboards, ten points for an ear, twenty for a nostril and so on (you have to be a pretty dab hand at darts to score a triple 20 underwater).

I have, however, left the best for last, the one irresistible detail which made Peter choose this schooner in preference to all the other sunken ships he had passed when swimming from the Neverland – and that is the fact that it came to rest on its mountain-side slightly aslant.

For has the child yet been born whose heart would not quicken at the thought of living in a house that *tilts*?

CHAPTER VI

Wet Land

The first thing Peter did when they arrived at the schooner was to show Miranda her quarters. The boys of the Brotherhood bunked down together, sleeping in hammocks with little belts that you fastened over the top to prevent you from floating away during the night – or sleep-swimming, as they called it. But Bee had to be different, and she had insisted on having a bedroom of her own; and it was now Peter's task to tell her that she would henceforth have to share with her newly arrived sister.

"I won't!" she screamed when he bluntly broke the news to her.

"You will!"

"Won't, I say!"

"Oh yes you will!"

"Oh no I won't!"

"Oh yes you will!"

To Miranda they sounded like two pantomime villains, and she could hardly refrain from joining in.

Then Bee attempted to stamp her foot in rage, a ploy that had always worked with her parents, but as she was drifting three feet above the floor at the time the result was pitifully ineffectual.

"But, Peter," she went on in her special wheedling voice, "it isn't fair. This is my room. Sisters should always have their own room. Besides, look at her," she said, pointing rudely at Miranda, "she's a great lump of a girl. She'll break all my things."

Bee was most terribly particular, you see, about her 'things': the doilies she crocheted herself and which covered every piece of her furniture; her extensive collection of shells, which she would take down in the evening and listen to as if they were gramophone records of the sea; and above all her clothes.

For she was a dressy little creature who would have gasped at the idea that she might appear in the same plant-wear *ensemble* two days swimming. She possessed a sarong for every conceivable social function, which meant that most of them were utterly impracticable for life at the bottom of the sea. Hanging neatly in rows on fish-bone clothes-hangers, they occupied every inch of space inside the wardrobe she was going to have to share with a room-mate.

Actually, if I mention all of this here, it's because I felt it might be desirable to change the subject as quickly as possible after Bee's unfortunate description of Miranda as "a great lump of a girl". Miranda had glared at Bee and spiritedly assured her that "anyway, she wouldn't touch her silly old things with a barge-pole", and requested her on pain of having her hair pulled to take back what she had said. It was Peter who finally brought an end to their foolishness by informing them that unless they made it up it was back to dry land for both of them.

"Well . . . all right," sniffled Bee, "but I won't have her near my Louis Quinze." (She pronounced 'Quinze' to rhyme with 'twins'.)

This was an exquisite Louis Quinze dressing-table Bee had had 'imported' from a French steamship which had foundered about ten leagues away. The reason she gave for not letting Miranda look in the gilt-framed mirror which was its centrepiece was that too many reflections might wear it out from overuse!

But Miranda did not mind very much, she was so enraptured with her new accommodation. And the fact that her sister was one of the most spoilt little girls she had ever come across, even among only children, was actually a secret source of pleasure to her, for it made her seem all the more 'family'. It may be hard to understand, but an only child misses the fighting and bickering of family life just as much as the affection.

In the days ahead she would grow to love her undersea home, especially the way everything in it was at an angle, so that when you climbed into your hammock at night it felt quite eerie to be horizontal for once. Yet how, you may ask, did they know when night had fallen? Perhaps I should have mentioned before that the mountain against which the ship rested was in reality a volcano that they had nicknamed 'Old Faithful'. Of course it was nearly extinct but it would obligingly begin to rumble every evening, and the glow from its red-hot core would light up the insides of the ship and make it snug and warm. Then by nine o'clock or thereabouts the rumbling would gradually die down again, so that was 'lights out'.

This, at least, was what Peter had told the children and what all of them loyally believed. It occurred to Miranda nevertheless, as it had occurred to the others in turn before they dismissed it from their minds, that it really happened the other way about. In short, at whichever hour of the day or night the volcano rumbled

– that became evening in Wet Land. Certainly it was exasperating to have just got up in the morning and be halfway through your breakfast when suddenly 'Old Faithful' would begin rumbling, the room would be bathed in an orangey, eveningy sort of glow and only a couple of hours later you would be climbing into your hammock again.

It would have been even more exasperating if you really went to bed at bed-time. But it was one of the strict rules of Wet Land that a full hour should elapse after lights out before anybody was to be found fast asleep. The Brotherhood, you see, was run according to a set of Spartan rules which everybody had to learn by heart on first arriving. These were, however, the complete opposite of the sort of regulations you would have to obey in a house or a school on land.

Thus, as I say, you had never to be caught going to bed when you were ordered to but romp about as rampagiously as possible for no less than an hour after lights out; pillow-fights had once been compulsory until they ran out of pillows. Then, it was expected of you at least once a week to grab the last oyster at dinner without first making sure that none of your brothers or sisters cared to have it. Again, if a football match had been organised, and it was your ball that day (for each of the children took it in turns to be the owner of the ball), and if the opposing team scored a goal from a position you just knew was offside but they insisted no less vehemently was not, then it was absolutely in order – indeed it was one of the most stringently observed rules of the game – to cry "It's my ball! Na! Na! Na! If you don't accept my decision I'll take it away and won't play any more!", and your adversaries had to yield. They may seem very easy rules to follow but I can assure you they were rigorously held to and anyone who broke one of them was severely punished. Punishment, by the way, consisted of being sent to Coventry, which meant in effect that you became an only child all over again. On the other hand, whatever the ragging that took place between them, no member of the Brotherhood was allowed to forget what it was that bound him to his fellows. If ever danger threatened from those creatures of the ocean that were just bursting with evil curiosity about the fascinating activity in and around the schooner, each of them knew that he must swim to the defence of a brother or sister without an instant's hesitation. From this powerful bond, it is said, we have the expression 'Blood is thicker than water'.

Miranda loved everything, the danger as well as the fun. She loved feeling beautifully cool all the day then rosily warm in the evening, smooth and slippery all over yet somehow never wet, since what makes the sea so magical a substance is that you are wet only when you rise to the surface.

So the time passed as though there were honey, not sand, in the hourglass. The days passed slowly, the weeks quickly, which is as it should be. And I think I could give you the most accurate picture of her new life by relating a typical day in Wet Land. But what day should I choose? What about last Tuesday? Last Tuesday is always a typical day, I have found, no matter who you are or where you live, with just enough of the out-of-the-ordinary to make it seem identical to all the others.

Well, last Tuesday began with Miranda dozily stirring in her hammock, wakened as usual by Bee's snoring. (Bee snored in a most ladylike fashion but, much as she would deny it, she did snore and the bubbles were there as proof.) Still a little drowsy, she unfastened her hammock belt, sneaked a glance at her reflection in the Louis Quinze, then swam out into the main stateroom.

Many of the children were still asleep; a few were already up and about making mud-pies all over the stateroom carpet, which was obligatory practice on Tuesday mornings; others were breakfasting on lava-grilled seaweed.

" 'Morning, Tom-Tom."

" 'Morning, Miranda."

" 'Morning, Bubbles."

" 'Morning, Miranda."

" 'Morning, Mortimer."

If no answer came this time it was because Mortimer was not one of the only children but a goldfish. It lived in its own bowl in the stateroom and it was Miranda's turn this morning to change the water. A goldfish may strike you paradoxically as a rather odd creature to encounter in the depths of the ocean – instead of in a living-room, I mean – but there was a perfectly simple explanation. Peter found the bowl while exploring his new home and decided that his Brotherhood should have a pet, a mascot, if you like. And what better mascot for an undersea Brotherhood of Only Children than a solitary goldfish swimming round and round in its bowl? So he searched about for a goldfish, christened it Mortimer and placed it inside the bowl. Now Mortimer was a dear little thing, and adored by everybody in Wet

Land, but he was somewhat simple-minded and it had never dawned on him that he could swim to his freedom any time he pleased. Or perhaps he simply preferred to remain where he was. Certainly, whenever one of the children was clumsy enough to knock over the bowl during a rag, as occurred daily, poor Mortimer would dutifully flounder about in a panic, his little gills athrob, just as if he were on some living-room carpet, until he was rescued and plopped safely back among his ferns and fish-eggs.

It was the same when it came to changing his water. Watch Miranda as she carefully dips her hand in the bowl so as not to frighten its timorous occupant. After a brief but frantic chase around the edge between her hand and Mortimer she manages at last to catch hold of him and drop him into a marmalade jar kept nearby for just such an emergency. Then she turns the bowl upside-down to drain off the stale water, gently transfers Mortimer back from his temporary to his permanent home and sprinkles some fresh fish-eggs over the surface.

But where was Peter? Not shinning up the ship's mainmast on a reconnoitring mission. (Actually, he could swim up just as well, but that was Peter all over.) Not riding his favourite pet dolphin in circles as though on a merry-go-round. Not, she knew, killing a shark – he never killed sharks as a rule before lunch. So where?

In the end she found him calmly playing scales on his pipes.

Miranda already knew what this meant. It meant that a new member was to be inducted into the Brotherhood. It was through the pipes, you see, that Peter or Ralph, whoever was in charge of the expedition, would utter the fateful phrase "It's a braw bricht moonlicht nicht the nicht". It was because of the pipes that the voice sounded so queer and disembodied.

She greeted him.

" 'Morning, Peter."

" 'Morning, Miranda," Peter replied between scales.

"You're practising on your pipes, I see."

" 'S'right."

"Is there a ship coming along this way?"

" 'S'right."

"But how is it you always know, Peter?"

"Easy. If you put your ear to the sea bed and you hear a far-off rumbling noise, that tells you a ship is approaching."

There was a pause.

"Peter?" Miranda ventured at last.

"Yes."

"Do you ever spare a thought for all the sorrowful mothers and fathers who must think their children have been eaten by sharks?"

"Never," he replied without hesitation.

"O Peter, how very heartless of you!"

"If they are foolish enough to mistake a lot of umbrellas for sharks' fins, that is their fault, I reckon, not mine."

She looked at him with reproach in her eyes.

"I say, Miranda, are you not happy here?"

"Ye-es," Miranda replied reluctantly, not because she was not but because it troubled her to admit it.

"Haven't I given you all the brothers you could ever wish for?"

"Yes, but—"

"The brothers you dreamt of having when you were alone in your nursery?"

"Oh yes, but—"

"Would you rather go back to being alone?"

"No," was Miranda's whispered reply; and it was the truth.

"You see!" cried Peter with a triumphant grin. "Brothers and sisters are good fun, but there's always a mother and father to spoil it. Here we have all the fun without any of the spoiling."

"But everybody needs a mother and father," Miranda answered a trifle pensively, for she realised just how little thought she had given lately to her own.

"Not I. I had a mother once. She left me and never came back. I shall never want another."

Because she had read the book about him Miranda knew that he was telling a fib, that it was he who had forgotten Wendy. But she only shook her head at him and asked, "Do you know, Peter, what somebody very famous once said?"

"Remind me," said Peter, who had never in his life been known to confess ignorance of anything and was not about to start now.

"No man is an island."

At these words a kind of shudder seemed to go through Peter's body, and he drew himself up to his full height of 4 feet 8 inches (with his shadow, you see, he had stood at 4 feet 9, which was the single thing he regretted about having torn it off).

"But, Miranda," he replied, with that terrifying smile of his which had the same effect on his friends as

"The moment finally came for her to inspect her new home."

Hook's hook had had on his enemies, "I *am* no man."

This, unfortunately, was Peter in one of his self-dramatising moods, as he was not really a callous little boy. It was just that he whizzed through life like a savage's arrow; and if an arrow were to pay the slightest heed to the people and the scenery which it passed it would doubtless miss its target. Peter could not have told you what the target of his life was but he was determined to hit the bull's-eye.

It was necessary to have that cleared up because we are about to witness an example of our hero at his most heedlessly cruel. For when Miranda innocently enquired if it was a girl he intended to recruit into the Brotherhood, Peter smiled with the smile of somebody who not only has the satisfaction of keeping a secret all to himself but the greater satisfaction of knowing that he is on the point of revealing it to another.

"Oh no," he whooped, "this time it must be a boy!"

"Why?"

He giggled wickedly. "Oh Miranda, I have had an idea for the most topping joke! It came to me when I decided it was time for Ralph to die."

"To die!" Miranda was horror-stricken.

"Well, not really and truly die, you know. But Ralph will have to return to dry land, and that's a bit like going up to Heaven."

"But why must he go?"

"His moustache!" cried Peter, suddenly cross.

"His *what*?"

"Moustache," answered Peter, who was none too pleased at having to repeat the horrid word. "Oh, it's a sly one, creeping along the corners of his mouth the way it does, but it's there all right. And having it breaks the most important rule of the Brotherhood. Ralph knows the rule, yet he deliberately disobeyed me." Peter shook his head in disbelief. "I didn't expect such treachery of my trusty second-in-command. Promise me, Miranda," he solemnly addressed her, "promise me you will never grow a moustache."

Miranda unhesitatingly promised. She was, however, still very anxious about Ralph's departure.

"But, Peter," she insisted, "he is your right hand, you need him more than all the rest of us."

"Why, there is no danger I cannot overcome by myself."

Brave words, Peter, words you will live to regret!

"But I haven't told you about my joke," he gleefully went on. "You see, when this new brother of ours dives into the ocean and we spirit him away, we'll leave Ralph there in his place! Oh, but can't you just see the faces of the mummy and daddy who will think their son has been saved then discover that it's another boy altogether!"

It saddens me to have to write that he turned an impudent somersault in front of Miranda, so enchanted was he with himself and his appalling little joke.

Miranda protested but she could not turn Peter aside from his intention: that selfsame morning he called a meeting of the whole Brotherhood to announce the fate which had been reserved for Ralph. For about five minutes the children showed a very real distress and I believe some of them shed real tears, although it is difficult to tell under the sea. Then, with the excitement of preparing for the excursion and arguing about what kind of new brother they hoped to acquire, they simply forgot that they were probably never going to see Ralph again.

As for Ralph himself, he flinched when he heard the decision but made no quarrel with it. For Peter was right in a sense: a few soft, downy hairs on his upper lip did indeed give the boy a manly quality that had never been there before, a quality not unlike the steadfastness that having a strong new chin imparted to the Major. He seemed to see Peter for the first time. He looked long and hard at the devil-may-care Pan, who was every-where at once – supervising the harnessing of the seahorse-and-carriage, playfully teasing Mortimer by tweaking his tail, thimbling one or two of the children just for the charm of it – and it may be that he suddenly felt a little too old for such careless childlike rompish-ness. I do not know, for he kept his own counsel. Ralph was the strong, silent type.

Except for a feeling of suppressed excitement at the prospect of the coming excursion, the rest of the morn-ing and afternoon were even more typical than is usual for a Tuesday.

Peter kept pretty much occupied until lunch-time, setting traps for mermaids. These were fearfully compli-cated affairs, constructed out of slatted wooden planks, pieces of rope all of different lengths, the figureheads of ships and, as bait, the aromatic plants on which mer-maids are said to dote. But although they looked as if they could not possibly fail to work, and they had at one time or another ensnared every single member of the Brotherhood – including, embarrassingly, Peter himself – no mermaid had ever been taken in. None of the children, in fact, had ever so much as caught a glimpse of one, and if only there had been an *Encyclopaedia Britannica* handy they could have consulted it and learned that the Indian Ocean is not at all a mermaid's habitat.

After lunch, in accordance with the Wet Land time-table, there was an hour of free time during which you were permitted to be on your own and do what you liked. Then, at 3 o'clock – that is to say, whenever Peter decided it might just as well be 3 o'clock – shark-hunting, which generally took them through to tea.

From time to time during the day Peter would break off from whatever he happened to be doing to put his ear to the ground and try to estimate how much longer it would be before the approaching steamer had reached them. Once or twice, because he was particularly busy, he asked Ralph to listen for him, quite forgetting that every knot the ship advanced brought Ralph that much nearer to his doom. Although there would be a searching look in his eyes, Ralph calmly did as he was asked; and when he reported back to Peter the latter amicably thanked him as if nothing whatsoever had changed.

Then the great moment arrived at last and the children impatiently set off in formation, their umbrellas tucked under their arms like huge black tulips that only blossom in the rain. Peter was in the vanguard, standing upright inside the umbrella-carriage and pretending to spur the seahorse on with a whip like a Roman centurion in his chariot; while Ralph, swimming slightly apart from the others, carried over his back a stick with a bundle tied to one end containing his few belongings. Of course he had sworn never to reveal to his eventual rescuers where he had been or with whom.

Up, up, upwards they swam. The whole ocean seemed to sway and surge to the engines of the ship that was drawing ever closer; and now the full moon was to be seen filtered through the layers of the sea like a lost florin glinting at one from the depths of a rock pool. This was Miranda's first trip of the kind, and she could hardly wait to discover what it felt like from a reverse angle, as they say in the moving pictures. Yet she was sad for Ralph, too, and would steal furtive glances at his impassive features.

But stay! With an imperceptible twitch of his fingers on the reins Peter drew the little seahorse up. There was

something above their heads; something moving on the surface of the sea; something that should not have been there. Everybody waited and listened and held their breath. Then suddenly they were given a surprise. To Miranda's eyes it was as if a drop of ink had trickled off the end of a pen-nib into a beaker of clear water and was starting to spread, loose and free, through the transparent liquid. A moment later she saw what it was exactly. The pen-nib was the hull of a small sailing-boat, the drop of ink a black pearl-fisher who had just gracefully plunged into the ocean.

"O the lovely!" she could not help exclaiming.

"Shhh!" signalled Peter. Then at a further signal from him the children hurriedly stuck the umbrellas down the front of their clothing and froze into immobility. (Thus did the plants of which that clothing was made serve as camouflage, a trick they picked up from many of the marine creatures around them.) They watched and waited till the diver had filled up his net with oysters and swum back to his boat. A minute or so later, however, there he was again, going briskly about his business.

Meanwhile the rumbling had become deafeningly loud. The ocean swelled and seethed and curdled. Still the diver filled his net with oysters and still the children held in their breath and endeavoured to look like plants.

Now the rumbles seem to be fading away and the sea has begun to settle again.

The ship has passed by. On board a little boy sleeps soundly, and his mother and father are no doubt tranquilly enjoying a lemon sole at dinner and remarking on what a smooth, uneventful voyage it has turned out to be. They have not the slightest notion of what an awfully narrow escape they have had.

Ralph has also, of course, had a narrow escape. Yet you might almost suppose Peter to be delighted that he would be staying on with the Brotherhood, moustache and all. More likely, though, he has already forgotten how Ralph was to have been abandoned. For on their return home he places his arm around the other's shoulder, as boys will, and gaily chatters to him about everything and nothing.

Nevertheless something has changed, even if Peter himself has no idea of it. Something in Ralph's eyes, especially when he looks at Peter, will never quite be the same again. And something, too, in Wet Land is never to be the same again, since on the very next day – but that, I think, must keep till the next chapter.

CHAPTER VII

Peter Recovers His Shadow

I sometimes think that if little children realised in the morning just how often they were going to burst into tears during the day they would be sorely tempted to stop in bed. Yet though they may have wept uncontrollably four or five times – because of a broken toy, perhaps, or a chafed elbow – by the evening most of them have to be dragged off to the nursery against their will and they scarcely seem able to wait for the next day to dawn. There were plenty of childish crises in Wet Land, too, although there the problem might be an old magnetic compass that had got cracked or a piece of shark-chop that had gone down the wrong way. But since underwater tears are invisible, nobody paid very much attention to them, and you could not on the whole have found a braver band of children east of Suez – or west, for that matter.

This also meant, however, that if one of them did cry so hard that you noticed, there was likely to be something genuinely amiss.

On the afternoon of which I speak (which is to say, on the day following their fruitless excursion) everything was apparently quite calm. It was the period of free time, so that all the children were engaged on various pursuits in and around the schooner. Peter himself was dozing in the upper fo'c'sle after an especially copious lunch and dreaming of – but not even an author has the right to trespass on his characters' dreams, and I have no idea of what he was dreaming. What I can tell you is that his were pleasant dreams, for there was a lovely crescent-moon smile on his face, just wide enough to permit the occasional bubble to peep out from his half-parted lips and make its leisurely way up to the surface.

Suddenly his siesta was disturbed by an ear-splitting shriek, which was then succeeded by a drawn-out and infinitely melancholic wail. Whereupon, as though fired from a cannon, he leapt to his feet and shot out through the port-hole.

Though none was as swift to it as Peter, the members of the Brotherhood immediately interrupted whatever they were doing and gathered round to find out what was causing the rumpus. As it came nearer and nearer, the wailing became louder and louder, until the very ocean seemed to ripple with grief. Who or what could it be?

"Oh rats!" cried Second Helping when the sufferer came into view. "It's only Bee."

"Yes," Miranda seconded him; "but look – what has happened to her?"

Bee came swimming towards them, a wobbly Bee none of them had ever seen before, although to begin with no one could make out the difference in her appearance.

Then Peter spoke.

"Her hair's been cut off," he declared portentously. Being the Brotherhood's chief scout as well as its leader, he had an eye for the telling detail.

"I think," Tom-Tom echoed him, "I think Peter's hit the nail on the head. Her hair's been cut off."

In fact, now that they had it pointed out to them, the difference struck the children as screamingly obvious. How could they have missed it? Bee's hair – the pride of her existence, the hair she tended with the same fond anxiety as a mother tending her child, the hair that so picturesquely streaked across her brow – was no more. Where once it had cascaded down her neck and lapped over her shoulders like a little golden waterfall there remained only ugly tufts. And no matter how aggravating she had been with her endless brushing and combing of it, it could not honestly be said that the new style was an improvement. If the truth be told, it looked as though it had been hacked off.

She went on wailing so, Peter was at last obliged to take her by the arms and give her quite a violent shake.

"Do buck up, Bee, and tell me what happened."

"I – I – I – whaa – whaa – whaa!"

"I know, Bee, I know," Peter murmured to her more gently, while he cradled her with unexpected tenderness. "But, you see, I cannot help you unless you tell me how it came about."

On another occasion you may be sure Bee would have taken full advantage of Peter's rarely accorded intimacy. Now she just calmed down a little, and although she continued to stutter, she managed to get her story out.

"I wasn't doing anything, Peter, really I wasn't. I had only g-g-gone out to comb my-my-my hair – it was the free period, after all, and I would have cleared the lunch things away – I really did mean to, later, and—"

"Yes, yes, we know you did, but what about your hair?"

"We-e-ll," said Bee tearfully, "it felt just as if somebody – or something – was watching me. I seemed to see – to see—"

"What?" everybody cried at once.

"Eyes!"

"Eyes?"

"Eyes!"

"Wh-wh-what happened next?" urged a trembling Bubbles, whose own eyes were as large as Portuguese oysters.

"Before I could escape," poor Bee went on, her hair (what was left of it) beginning to stand on end at the horrible memory of it all, "I was attacked by a – a—"

The silence was even louder than the wailing had been.

"A crocodile!"

A crocodile?

It was a much relieved Bubbles who now offered his considered opinion on the subject. "Aw, hooey!" he cried, blowing a scornful bubble on his air-plant. "Ain't no such thing as crocodiles in the sea!"

The children looked at each other with sheepish expressions. Why, of course there were no such things as crocodiles in the sea. Crocodiles, as everybody knew, were only to be found in rivers.

"But there are no such things as little children in the sea," Bee countered, with something of her natural contrariness, "yet here we are."

The children again fell a-trembling. O true, there should be no such things as little children in the sea, yet there they were nevertheless.

Everybody turned to Peter, who had been strangely quiet since Bee spoke. For mention of a crocodile had rung a bell in his head, and that bell was the bell of an alarm clock. Could it be? No, no, that life was gone, dead and buried, ancient history. And yet . . . Here was a puzzle.

"What are we to do? Tell us, Peter!" The cry arose on every side.

"Do?" repeated Peter, and he actually had a smile on his face as he said it. "We are to take Bee inside and comfort her and tend to her hair. That is what we are to do."

"But – the crocodile, Peter?"

"You have all heard Bubbles," he answered briefly. "There are no crocodiles in the sea. But if you like," he added with characteristic nonchalance, "we shall post a guard on the ship this night."

That is what happened. The first night's guard was Second Helping; and as the others settled down in their hammocks he rested his back comfortably – in the event, too comfortably – against the hull of the schooner to watch and wait.

Now, when the atrocity took place in the middle of the night, and Peter and the children hastened to his defence, Second Helping had a perfectly reasonable explanation. If he had closed his eyes – and, mind you, it was only for a second or two – then it was in order to hear the better, for it's a well-known fact that the blind are possessed of a wonderfully acute sense of hearing. The next thing he knew, however, was that he was being pinioned by a dozen pairs of hands while another hand was prising open his mouth and pouring into his throat a thick, viscous liquid which, if he had not known it to be an impossibility, he could have sworn was castor oil. He too, his ordeal at an end, had seemed to see a crocodile's tail go whish-whish-whishing into the night.

Then, having accounted for his side of the story, he hurriedly took his leave and did not reappear till lunch-time the following day, where he looked like a slightly wrinkled beach ball from which the air had been let out, and refused a second helping for the first time in human memory.

The Brotherhood went on the alert. Peter, now in his element, could scarcely contain his excitement. An enemy was abroad, and if there was one thing that pleased him better than a friend it was an enemy. But first a plan had to be formulated; and the very next evening, when the schooner glowed crimson from the volcano so that it looked from the outside like a whale that had been gutted to make a giant's Hallowe'en lantern, Peter put forth his plan.

"What we need is a decoy," he announced to the semi-circle of upraised, flickeringly illumined faces.

"What is a decoy?" Miranda asked.

"Bait," was Peter's answer. "Crocodile bait. I shall lie in ambush for this crocodile" – he spat out the word with all the contempt he could muster – "if crocodile it be. But there must be bait to lure the beast in, and that will be the decoy. Volunteer?"

There came an intense silence to Wet Land, and you would have said that everybody's feet had been rooted to the spot except that, of course, there was no spot to be rooted to in the ocean.

Then above that silence was heard a voice.

"I shall be the decoy," said Ralph.

"Nay, Ralph," replied Peter. "I thank ye for volunteering, but nay." (Whenever the fever of adventure was upon him Peter would instinctively start to employ words like 'nay' and 'ye'.)

"Why not?"

"Because you are tall and strong – our crocodile mightn't decide to attack you. Besides, if the plan went wrong, I could not afford to lose my trusty second-in-command."

"Naturally not," said Ralph, dazed by Peter's awful cynicism. "You could not afford to lose your trusty second-in-command."

But Peter was oblivious to the bitter irony in Ralph's words. "It must be," he went on, "somebody little and helpless. Otherwise it would not be proper bait."

"Then let it be me."

Who spoke? It was Miranda.

"You?" cried Peter. "But you are a mere girl."

"All the more reason."

"You will probably be afraid."

"Then the crocodile will catch the scent of my fear and be attracted by it."

"The risk is great."

"Not when you are lying in ambush, Peter."

This proved to be the conclusive argument. Peter, who feared no man, became soft putty in the hands of a flatterer. Miranda was to be the decoy.

While the children they were leaving behind peered out at them, bright-eyed and fearful, through the ship's port-holes, Peter and Miranda departed to set the trap. So silently and discreetly did they glide, even stealth itself could be dispensed with: they gave the impression of swimming on tiptoe.

The spot chosen for the ambush was the same coral rock on which Peter had been standing when Miranda first saw him. Now it was her turn to lie across it, as if fast asleep. With her white night-gown spread out at her feet (for it was only when their own clothes had all but crumbled away that the children of the Brotherhood would weave new ones out of sea-plants) she looked so frail and wraith-like that a host of tiny fish were already swarming nosily about her recumbent figure. Peter, meanwhile, concealed himself nearby, his pearl-handled knife poised to strike.

He waited.

The ocean was calm and still, almost as though it were asleep on its own bed; as though all the little denizens of the deep were nestled together in slumber, head to tail, like sardines in a can.

And he waited.

The wan moon shed a watery glow down into the profundities of the sea like a street-lamp glimmering through a London pea-souper, and still he waited. Indeed he waited for such a time that he became no longer sure whether Miranda was pretending to be asleep or had actually dozed off from boredom.

Suddenly, dotted about the reef, a dozen sleeping little fish opened their eyes. Or rather, the little fish *were* eyes: the rocks on which they had seemed to be resting were heads, the reeds that an instant before had been undulating around these rocks were hair and the queerly shaped shadows playing over the sand were bodies. Peter squeezed his fingers tight on the pearl of his knife-handle. But for the moment he remained motionless. For something was slithering obscenely across the sea bed, something which certainly resembled a crocodile, which had a crocodile's skin and a crocodile's tail. Except that, just when you were absolutely convinced that it was indeed a crocodile, it did what no crocodile in Christendom is able to do – it stood up on two hind legs!

Peter, I have to say, was not cowed but thrilled by the apparition. Thrilled to the core of his being. What even he could never have dared to hope was then true after all. Leaping out from his hiding-place he set himself squarely between Miranda and the evil, unnatural thing.

"So!" he cried out in a voice that sent shivers through the whole Indian Ocean. "So, we meet again, foul creature!"

The crocodile reared its head with a vicious snarl. Then with what appeared at first glance to be a claw but revealed itself on closer acquaintance to be a hook it lashed out furiously at the impetuous boy.

Peter nimbly danced to escape it, so nimbly you might have supposed he danced with joy. For he had recovered his shadow. Oh, not that paltry, paper-thin excuse for a shadow that Wendy had sewn back on! The shadow of his life, the shadow of which he was the refulgent light.

You will already have guessed, Reader. This was no crocodile, this was Captain Jas. Hook himself, late of the Neverland!

" 'Ralph will have to return to dry land.' "

CHAPTER VIII
Hook's Story

S ince no more than a second elapsed before the indefatigably vile ex-buccaneer lashed out at Peter with his iron claw, I had better make speedy work of my description of him.

It was, in his purely physical aspect, very much the Hook of yore. There could be seen the same slightly sinister elegance in his bearing, the same permanent rictus of disdain on his handsome countenance, as if his fleshly lips had performed the commission of sneering for him so often they henceforth knew no other posture of repose, the same two fiery red pinpoints which would highlight his blue eyes if ever he were crossed. And, of course, that hook – his *arm* in both senses of the word, not so much a weapon as an organic part of his body – from which derived his hideous appellation. Oh, this was Hook all right, no mistake!

Gone, however, was the Charles II finery he had earlier affected, those flounces and ruffles that had lent him an oddly feminine appearance among his filthy crew. Hook's new attire was a crocodile-skin suit, as impeccably cut as if it had been entrusted to Savile Row's finest tailor. His face fitted snugly between the beast's open jaws: its head and upper jaw, worn at a rakish angle on Hook's own head, made for a wonderfully dashing hat not unlike an Admiral's; as for the lower jaw, jutting out from under Hook's chin, it served as a dainty ruff collar of teeth instead of lace. And, there having always been a touch of the dandy in his make-up, Hook had actually contrived to run up a sort of lapel buttonhole on the crocodile's belly, in which was inserted a sickly-hued sea-anemone whose legs would snap shut on any unwary fish that swam too close. (On very special occasions he would sport a matching one over his left ear.)

Such was James Hook as he presented himself now to Peter; but before you could say 'Jack Robinson' or even just 'Jack' he lunged at the child's vulnerable little Adam's apple with his hook.

"Well, Pan," he hollered, "it is we two again – just as in the good old days!"

"That it is, cap'n," replied Peter with an ironic emphasis on the man's usurped rank, while he darted aside to avoid the hook's serpent-tooth point, "and I thank the Heavens for according me the pleasure of polishing you off a second time."

"Oho, you young gutter rat!" laughed Hook, advancing towards Peter on crocodile-skin moccasins (in an incongruously flat-footed fashion, it has to be owned). "This is no ghost that stands before you, Peter Pan. It would take a better man than you to come within *that*" – he snapped his fingers, but failed to obtain the requisite snapping sound under the sea – "of killing James Hook and living to tell the tale. And if anybody is soon to be engaged on a polishing chore, 'tis I!"

He mistimed his second blow, which was apparently intended to split Peter's head in two, and came to a halt bent double with the exertion. Whereupon Peter comically wriggled through his open legs and popped up behind him. So neat was the manoeuvre on both sides, in fact, it was almost as though it were a game, as though the intoxication of the renewed encounter were such that they hoped to prolong the pleasantries for as long as possible.

Hook, however, did not care much to be an object of ridicule; and with a grimace he turned upon Peter, lashing out tirelessly to right and left.

"Aren't you even passing curious, O scum of the sea, to learn how I chance to be here?" he enquired with that ghastly parody of good manners for which he had been famed the length and breadth of the Barbary Coast.

"Indeed I am, thou abominable monstrosity!" Peter replied no less graciously. "But first let me satisfy my curiosity on another matter that used to plague me. Your good arm seems to be a trifle itchy."

"Itchy?" Hook echoed blankly.

"Yes. So you won't mind if I scratch it for you."

Before the momentarily puzzled Hook could answer, Peter leapt forward with his pearl-handled knife then, almost tenderly, ripped through the crocodile-skin sleeve the pirate had woven for himself and drew his blood.

"So," said Peter, pretending to appear chastened. "Forgive my unworthy suspicions. It *is* blue, after all."

It was true. Hook's blood, already forming a tiny rosette on his clothing, was of a deep aristocratic blue, precisely the shade claimed to be that of – but no, the family I was about to name is still one of the most powerful and influential in the land, and I should risk finding myself sued for libel if I were to implicate it here on the basis of such flimsy evidence.

"Odds, bobs, hammer and tongs!" screeched Hook, who disliked having his own blood publicly aired even more than he enjoyed doing the airing where other people's blood was concerned. "For that trick I'll dice you into forty little cubes and feed you to your own goldfish, that I will!"

"Before making the dish you'll have to prepare the ingredients," crowed Peter, leapfrogging over Hook's head. "But you were going to tell me how you came to be here in one piece."

"Aye, you imagined you had seen the last of your old enemy, did you not? But no, this hook o' mine, that I would be unhappier to lose than my good arm, saved me then as it has done so often. It caught in the crocodile's mouth, don't you know, just as though it were a-dangling from a fisherman's rod! Ha! Ha! Ha!" His laugh would have chilled the blood of Old Nick himself. "Oh dear me, the poor helpless creature thrashed this way and that, try as he might he couldn't swallow me – little fish-bone got stuck in his throat, ye might say!"

"What happened next?" asked Peter, who almost against his will had become extremely interested.

But in his curiosity he relaxed his vigilance for a crucial instant, thus allowing Hook in his turn to gash him lightly on the chest. Peter bit his lower lip and managed not to cry.

"Why, Hook, you're tickling me!"

"Aye, and with my next blow I'll tickle ye from the inside out. We'll see if that makes ye laugh as heartily! But to continue –" he went on in a more neutral, informative tone of voice, "– there was I, installed inside the beast's gullet, though not the ideal tenant, I can tell you. Oh, I would scratch 'im and I would tickle 'im and when I remembered what that crocodile had done to me I would twist my hook nicely up into the lid of his mouth – that set his tail a-spinning!" The two of them were lunging and parrying wellnigh absent-mindedly, it was second nature to them now. "It wasn't a bad sort of life while it lasted, I should say; a man could grow soft inside a crocodile's belly. The bedding was comfortable, the heating was always at room temperature, there was plenty to eat – lots of delicious little fishes would come straying our way, and I took my share of them before my landlord got his. I'm not ashamed to confess I shed a few tears when he finally gave up the ghost on me."

While feigning to sympathise with him, Peter thrust at the man's swarthy features with his knife.

"Naughty, naughty," said the Captain, wagging his hook at him in mock admonishment. "You'll have to rise a deal earlier in the morning, Pan, to catch me so easily. Well, as I was saying, I had got rather fond of that old croc's insides and decided to make myself a suit out of his skin. And because the iron of my hook was tending to weigh me down (or mayhap it was the iron in my soul at the notion of your swimming about free and unfettered) I taught myself to live in this new element, as you have done."

"Rot!" Peter witheringly retorted. "I didn't have to learn. Peter Pan *is* an element, just as water is. We have much in common, the ocean and I."

That, of course, was utter nonsense, but it had the desired effect of making Hook gnash his teeth in frustration. Was he always to be bettered in repartee by this callow child? It really was too bad.

"Maybe so," Hook replied darkly, "and then again maybe not. But since I have conquered the ocean I shall not take long to conquer you."

"To be sure, you aren't alone," said Peter cuttingly. He had become aware of several pairs of eyes glinting narrowly at him out of the darkness. "Will you not introduce me to your friends?"

"Of course, of course," Hook practically cooed. "All in good time. First, though, I must tell you whence they come. Picture me, then, swimming about with no project in mind, when suddenly the ocean starts to boil above my head. What mischief is this? I ask myself. I rise to the surface, and there, no more than half a league distant, what do I spy with my little eye? A vessel bound for Davy Jones' locker! Oh, the pretty picture it made. And Hook's Luck was with me still. For know ye what this ship contained? Only a cargo of bully boys – the worst from every public school and crammer in England – to be shipped off to Australia by special decree of the King. But these were no ordinary school bullies, the sort that's expelled for forcing one of their fellows to swallow chalk or roasting another to a turn over a spit. Nothing as namby-pamby as that. Tupman here," he said, his hook indicating a villainous youth with a monocle tightly screwed into one eye, "Tupman here burned down his school, only it still had half the masters inside it. And Pincher, now, he made the littlest boy in his house drink a whole bucket of tar just because he disagreed with him. Tar disagreed with him too, poor fellow! Quite a card in his way is Pincher. As for Mouse Minor" – this of a tiny prodigy of cruelty with the face of a baby ferret – "well, I should prefer not to mention the prank he got up to; not in front of a lady," he added, leering evilly at Miranda. "The other lads have their specialties too, as I mean you to discover in due course. And then – wait for it, Pan, for this is the best of all – who should be their chaperone aboard ship but a dear old acquaintance of yours. Step forward, Smee, and greet our friend here."

Smee, Hook's bos'n of old, emerged from the shadows and gave Peter a sideways smile.

" 'Evening, Master Peter," he murmured in his soft Irish brogue. "Small world, ain't it?"

Smee, who once throttled his grandmother for a bet, had never been one to hold a grudge.

"Why, Smee," said Peter at his most ingratiating, "I swear I should have missed you had you not been at Hook's side."

"Thank you, young sir," Smee answered in kind. "I appreciate your putting it that way."

"Bah!" snarled Hook, who had evidently grown impatient with this agreeable banter. "A pox on such fooling and pretending!" He drew back from Peter and raised his hook above him as if taking an oath. "I give you warning, Peter Pan, I will tear you into ribbons yet, you and every milksop who stands behind you. Spread the word through the ocean that Hook is abroad and that naught but the sanguine rum will quench his thirst! For 'tain't only friends but enemies too who know how to solemnise a pact in blood," he cried, ruefully inspecting the gash in his arm then cheering up at the sight of the red rose in the buttonhole of Peter's wound, "and that is what you and I have done this night."

With these words he turned on his heels, followed by

his new-mustered crew; and if again the effect was a trifle spoiled by the ungainly manner in which the crocodile-suit obliged him to waddle, Hook had nevertheless made his point.

CHAPTER IX

Hook at Bay

Following the events related in the last chapter, Hook and his men returned to their own lair, a dank undersea cavern located about a league from the ship. There they spent the remainder of the night in drunken carousal, indulging in such charming pastimes as blowing up turtles till they burst like balloons and chopping live eels into tiny, wriggly pieces. I say 'they', but I do not include Hook or Smee, who were of an older and wiser generation than their underlings and who, in fairness to them, had scant relish for such childish barbarities. Smee, much taken by the plant-wear of the only children, was placidly sewing for himself a costume out of similar material. Indeed, watching his needle go clickety-clack, you would have said he was as accustomed to handling it as a cutlass. As for Hook, he lay curled up in a corner of the cave musing on the great and hopeless paradox of all arch-enemies.

Yes, there were times when Hook was more to be pitied than feared! Pitied, that black-hearted sea-dog? Aye, pity him, Reader, that put-upon pirate! You have heard of unrequited love? Well, his was a tragic case of unrequited hate. For somewhere dark and deep in his innards Hook was eaten up by the suspicion that Peter *did not truly hate him*, Peter whom he hated as he had never hated anyone in his life before, Peter whose soul

he would have liked to skewer from his body like a cork from the neck of a bottle.

Hook savagely yanked the sea-anemone from his buttonhole and began to pull off its legs one by one. "He hates me – he hates me not. He hates me – he hates me not. He hates me – he hates me not! Oh, I knew it to be so: he hates me not!" Like all buccaneers he was awfully superstitious.

The thing had become crystal-clear. Peter hated him the way a child thinks he hates the actor playing the villain in a pantomime, with an intensity that is itself a kind of play-acting. And if the boy had often tried to kill him, it was only because he would have felt silly merely booing him. In truth he had been as delighted to see his old enemy as a child is, though he knows it not, when the villain slinks on to the stage and twirls his mustachios. Confronted with Hook in his crocodile-suit, Peter's bright little eyes, instead of widening in terror or narrowing with disgust as they were supposed to do, had lit up with joy!

"I swear it!" Hook said to himself, but aloud, as if he were talking in his sleep. "I swear I saw his eyes light up!"

"Whose eyes?" asked Smee, removing some pins from his mouth.

"Why, Pan's, of course!" cried an exasperated Hook. "Do you know, the brat was actually glad to see me!"

"Oh, I doubt that, captain," Smee pleasantly remarked after a moment's reflection. "Who would ever be glad to see *you*?"

"Eh, what's that?" growled Hook.

"Why, captain, I had always understood," said Smee, "that you wanted to be universally hated, loathed, detested and abominated."

"Well . . . naturally I do. But that is just what I complain of. I want it most of that boy – but does he hate me, Smee, really and truly? That is the question."

"I would swear on my white-haired old grandmother's head that he does."

"Are you being honest with me, scug?"

"As honest as the day is long," the bos'n answered, blinking angelically behind his spectacles.

(Neither of them, fortunately, realised that the date was the 21st of December, the shortest day of the year.)

"I am something to that boy," Hook went on, "but I know not what exactly. Often-times I fancy he treats me as a – as a" – he could hardly bring himself to pronounce the word – "as a *toy*. Odds blood, I won't stand for being a child's living plaything!"

"You are his arch-enemy, in my opinion," said Smee, carefully examining a stitch.

His arch-enemy! That was it. Every hero had his arch-enemy, his very own whom he refused to share with anybody else. Sherlock Holmes, for instance, had Professor Moriarty; and although by all accounts this Moriarty was an evil genius whose malevolent shadow was cast just about everywhere, nobody but Holmes seemed troubled by it. None of the other Great Detectives in the world, after all, had ever come up against his handiwork, just as he, Hook, was destined never to pit his wits against Holmes. Arch-enemies, it appeared, were eternally bound to one another like Siamese twins. That was fair enough, but why, oh why, did he have to be Peter Pan's?

Hook sighed.

"What's the matter, captain?" Smee complacently enquired.

"I tell thee, Smee, when Peter made me walk that plank aboard the old *Jolly Roger*, and that crocodile rolled out the red carpet of his tongue to greet me, I hated him more than I have ever hated any living thing."

"I believe you, captain."

"Afterwards, when I went back to the Neverland and discovered he had gone, I could not stomach the idea that I'd been kept alive only to have him escape me again. I swore to myself, by Hook or by hook, I swore, I will track down that child and rid myself of his accursed interfering once and for all!"

"I know you will do."

"Aye, Smee, indeed I will, for there is inside o' me a silver compass whose needle always points to success. But the question is – what does it all mean? Aye, there's the rub."

Not being an intellectual, Smee could no longer follow Hook's philosophical speculations, and patiently waited for him to answer his own query.

"'Twas hatred of Peter Pan kept me alive, 'twas hatred of him drew me to this spot – why, 'tis hatred makes the world go round! But that hatred will be the death of one of us, and then what? If I kill Peter what will become of me?"

Though I put it inside inverted commas this last question, as it happens, proved too embarrassing to be spoken out loud. Hook merely posed it inwardly. But since Smee was still waiting for him to complete his train of thought Hook did speak at last, phrasing the same question a little differently.

"I mean, *when* I kill Peter what will I have left?"

Smee, who did not understand that the question was rhetorical, which means it was to be left hovering and unanswered, pondered it for a few seconds, then said in a wishing-to-be-helpful voice, "You'll have me. You'll have your boys."

"You!" Hook spat. "The boys! Pah!"

Now Smee was in a huff. "I'm right sorry, captain, right sorry you should take it that way," he mumbled. "I'm sure I've always tried to do my best for you. As for the lads there, why, they worship the very water you tread on."

"Belay that sulking, Smee, or I'll give ye something truly to sulk about."

But Hook made this threat distractedly, his mind was elsewhere. A thought had entered his fevered brain, a thought even more frightful than those already haunting it, an unthinkable thought. Could it be . . . No, no, no, change the subject, change the subject, think of something else! But could it be . . . I tell you, I shan't listen, shan't, shan't, shan't, shan't! But could it be that, in some strange and inexplicable fashion, he and Peter were two of a kind, soaring far, far above the petty creatures, the minnows, who swarmed around them? That after all they were *on the same side*?

For someone who had devoted his whole life to the destruction of Peter Pan, that was going too far, even for a thought surfacing briefly in the dark night of his black soul. Hook pulled himself together.

"Tomorrow, Smee—"

"Yes, captain?" said Smee keenly, relieved to see new colour in his master's face and hear new strength in his voice.

"Tomorrow," bellowed Hook, "the campaign begins proper. And I want those landlubbing bilge-rats of yours to remember every sort of nastiness they ever got up to, I want them to imagine all sorts of nastinesses they'd never have dared to get up to before, I want them to have every infant in Pan's crew cursing his parents for ever bearing him, d'ye hear?"

"I do that, captain."

"And, Smee—"

"Yes, captain?"

You could tell how passionately Hook felt about the question by the beads of sweat that glistened on his brow, for it is no easy matter sweating under the sea.

"Above all, I want Peter Pan left to my devices."

"Yes, captain."

"Peter," said Hook, "is mine."

CHAPTER X

First Blood

Of course Peter and Miranda had meanwhile returned to the ship, where the children were waiting to hear their account of the night's doings. Although it was long past hammock-time, even for Wet Land, the smallest ones had been allowed to stay up specially; and since 'Old Faithful' had ceased its rumblings, so that there was hardly any light inside the stateroom, all that could be made out were pairs of little eyes wide open in anticipation of some new terror. In fact their terror was so much more acute before Peter's return because they were still sickeningly uncertain whether he would come at all, and a few of the older rascals caused them to scream with fright by assuring them that he had probably been gobbled up, bones and everything, by the crocodile. There are drawbacks, too, in having brothers and sisters.

At least their worst fears had been spared when the two little ambushers came swimming towards them. They were safe. They were sound. They had not been gobbled up by the crocodile. Their hair appeared to be the same length as when they had set out. Oh happy day!

"The crocodile, Peter?" they clamoured around him.

Before replying, Peter hesitated an instant (purely for effect). "There is no crocodile," he said at last, as though that were an end to the matter.

"The two of them were lunging and parrying."

No crocodile? Oh joyous, joyous day!

"However . . ." he added, with that same ingrained sense of the dramatic pause.

However? What means this however?

"There is Hook. Captain James Hook. The only man whom Barbecue feared, and Flint himself feared Barbecue. *The* Hook," he stressed, distinguishing him from all the less notorious Hooks who might also be roving the Indian Ocean.

There was a fearful silence. The older children were afraid because they had once thrilled to stories of Hook under the bed-clothes when pretending to be asleep, and the younger children were afraid because the older children were afraid.

This was such stuff as rude awakenings are made on.

"He was alone, was he?" asked Tom-Tom, masking his dread of Peter's answer by a veneer of detachment.

"No."

"Had his men about him, had he?"

"Hadn't he just!"

"Roughly, you know, how many?"

" 'Bout fifteen, I should say," Peter replied.

"Did you," Tom-Tom huskily enquired, "say fifteen or fifty?"

"Fif*ty*," said Peter, enunciating more clearly to make himself understood.

"Pirates all, I suppose?"

"Bullies," answered Peter with a spine-chilling terseness. "School bullies."

School bullies! Then indeed the children shuddered, and some of them started to cry. For whereas, if viewed in a certain light, pirates were rather jolly, colourful creatures, who wore the kinds of clothes they would have liked to wear and had the enviable gift of being able to carry knives between their teeth without chapping their lips or getting the toothache, school bullies represented an enemy most of the only children already had cause to fear. If such a thing as a questionnaire had been handed around, and they had been invited to list in order of importance their reasons for preferring life under the sea, many of them, I believe, would have written "Because there are no bullies" in first position.

"This is a story, isn't it?" asked Tom-Tom, assailed as he was by memories of being debagged at school and having toothpaste squeezed under his bed-covers while he was asleep. "I mean to say, this is just one of those book stories, and we will all go back to bed and forget about it. I generally like such stories," he added doubtfully.

"No," said Peter in an indignant tone, "it is not a story!"

"Except," Miranda interposed, "for the part about there being fifty men." Even underwater she had her feet firmly on the ground.

"Why, Miranda, you fibber!" cried Peter. "There *were* fifty – fifty if there was one."

"Well, Peter Pan! It's you who are the fibber," said Miranda daringly. "Besides, you know you cannot count over ten."

Peter suddenly looked as if he were going to cry. "There were lots," he said resentfully. "Lots. Fifty means lots, doesn't it?"

"Ye-es ... it does," Miranda replied after a pause, when she saw how easy it was for Peter to lose face in front of the children. She particularly did not want to embarrass him at such a tense and difficult moment. "Of course, I know you are right," she whispered conspiratorially to him. "I only meant that you should try not to frighten the little ones."

"Good thinking," Peter whispered back; then, head hung low as if he were nobly sacrificing his reputation for the sake of the common cause, he addressed them all. "Perhaps I was wrong. Perhaps there weren't *quite* as many as fifty."

Peter, you must realise, had not really sought to frighten them – it was just that he had got into the regrettable habit of exaggerating a little when recounting his past exploits, and he had forgotten that in this instance everybody was personally concerned.

Somehow, though, his contrite admission of error had not sounded wholly convincing. For the very first time there could be heard in Wet Land those age-old laments of the lonely and unhappy child: "I want to go home" and "I want my mummy" (even if for the moment they were only spoken *sotto voce*).

Peter therefore decided to assume his most commanding manner and make a speech.

"Listen now, all of you," he said in a voice that immediately calmed their fears. "This is no time for moans and groans. This is a time to remember that we are all brothers and sisters, and that nobody is an only child in the Brotherhood of Only Children. When you were bullied at school you had no brothers or sisters to defend you, as you have now. You had no Peter Pan to defend you, as you have now. I have crossed swords with this Hook before, and he does not scare me. I have killed him before, and I can do it again. You want to go home, do you? Would you not first be heroes? Well, heroes ride runaway horses – and Hook's gang of ruffians is the runaway horse that we shall ride and we shall tame! Who rides with Peter Pan?"

"Me! Me! Me! Me! Hurrah for Peter!"

But three voices were missing from the cry of triumph. Bee's, because ever since she had been attacked by Hook and his bullies she had lived a life of total reclusion, with the shades pulled down in her bedroom and her Louis Quinze mirror permanently veiled until her thick, lustrous curls should have grown back again. Ralph's, because, young as he still was, something had died inside him ever since he had been betrayed by Peter. The death had gone quite unremarked by the person responsible for it, but it had occurred nevertheless. And Second Helping's, because – but that's right, where was Second Helping?

Since it might be best if his whereabouts remained a secret from Peter himself, who would have been absolutely furious to hear what he had been up to, I am prepared to tell you only in the strictest confidence. (And if you wish to pass it on, inform no more than one person at a time, for that is what a secret is.)

It so happened that Second Helping was addicted to midnight snacks, a bad habit he had picked up at boarding-school. Unknown to the others he would slip out from the schooner as soon as his tummy told him it was twelve o'clock, and his tummy was usually so accurate you could have set your clock by it, then swim off to the nearest oyster-bed, where all the oysters lay snugly tucked up together. There he would gather up as many of them as his plump little hands could hold and find for himself some nice, quiet spot on the surface of the sea to enjoy them.

Now, save when a new member was being recruited, the surface was strictly out-of-bounds to the only children; and although, as we saw, many of the rules of the Brotherhood were actually made to be disobeyed, this was one which none of the other members had ever dreamt of breaking. But since oysters have such a very oceany flavour it was Second Helping's opinion that they simply had no taste at all if consumed under the sea. So night after night you might have observed him contentedly floating about on the surface of the Indian Ocean, prising open the oyster-shells with his knife and, after tossing away any pearls he might have found, letting their delicious insides go slithering down his throat. Naturally they would have tasted nicer still with lemon juice and a few slices of brown bread and butter, but then you can't have everything.

Not even his anxiety to learn what might have happened to Peter and Miranda was enough to break the habit of a lifetime; and he expected, anyway, to have returned long before they did.

As I say, there he was, popping one oyster after another into his mouth, when, without any warning, he felt two cold, clammy hands draw him under the water and down into its depths.

"Well, well, well," he heard somebody say, "look what we 'ave 'ere, Tupman. 'ook won't 'alf be pleased."

"Oh, I say there," drawled Tupman, screwing his monocle more tightly into his eye, "didn't you hear the Captain? We start the campaign tomorrow."

" 'Tis tomorrow. After midnight, ain't it?"

"Hmm, true enough, Pincher. True enough."

It was Tupman and Pincher, who had forsaken the merry-making of their fellows to seek out more exquisite forms of mischief. Initially their ambitions had risen no higher than the dismemberment of a crab or the torturing of a stickleback, so that they could scarcely credit their good fortune when they spied Second Helping, who, as if true to his name, was about to receive his second helping of their boyish high spirits. Here was a prey worthy of a little inventive villainy.

"What'll it be, then, Tupman?" Pincher gleefully demanded of his smirking companion.

"Let me see now," said the other, giving Second Helping's arm a vicious twist while he pondered that interesting question. "This one's so awfully soft and round, he's rather like an air balloon, isn't he?"

"Ow, rawther!" said Pincher, giggling senselessly at his own imitation of Tupman.

"Then p'raps if we pricked him he might burst. Messy but fun, what?"

"Oi'll say," cried Pincher, who was already rubbing his hands together in expectation of both the mess and the fun.

With all the strength that lay buried deep beneath his layers of fat Second Helping screamed for help. He first screamed for Peter and then, at the very last, he screamed for his mother. After that, he just screamed.

What ensued is so horrible to relate that the quicker it is disposed of the better it will be. The two bullies looked about for the very sharpest and prickliest of plants. Then, while Tupman held Second Helping fast on the ocean floor, Pincher proceeded to stick its thorns one by one into the tenderest areas of his body. After an hour or so of such treatment poor Second Helping, when he returned stumblingly to the ship, looked like nothing so much as a hedgehog, or like Sebastian, the patron saint of hedgehogs. His only consolation was that in all the fuss that was made of him nobody remembered to ask where he had been and what he had been doing.

First blood to Hook! Peter ground his teeth in rage. As Miranda delicately removed the thorns from Second Helping's flayed and martyred flesh – though not delicately enough, oh no, it could never be delicately enough! – he faced the assembled children.

"This," he grimly declared, "means war."

"Yes, Peter!" they cried.

"Are you with me?"

Need he ask?

"Then this you must promise me."

"Yes, Peter?"

"None of you takes on Hook, is that understood?"

"Whatever you say, Peter!" they promised him. It was an order nobody felt the least inclination to question.

"Hook," said Peter, "is mine."

CHAPTER XI

Peter is Carried Off

The observation that it's always darkest before the dawn is one with which a condemned man, due to be hanged the following morning at 6 sharp, might beg to differ, but it generally tends to hold good. The night before a battle, for instance, is especially propitious to fitful slumber and incomprehensible but ill-boding dreams, and that preceding the engagement about to pit Peter and the only children against Hook and his gang of bullies was no exception. Thus the smaller ones in the Brotherhood slept two, sometimes three, to a hammock, looking just like a litter of pups in a basket; and even if such arrangements resulted in more of them than usual floating away in the night and having bothersomely to be retrieved by the others the way a gentleman scurries after his hat when it blows off in a gale, there was, they felt, something about the softness and warmth of another throbbing little body beside your own that compensated for all the inconvenience.

As for Peter, he was in the stateroom poring over useless but impressive-looking maps and timetables, devising a plan of defence for the morrow. Because of Second Helping having overheard Tupman and Pincher speak of it, he knew that that was when Hook intended to attack. But it was an awkward business all the same. Hook was such an underhanded strategist you never knew precisely where you stood with him. Certainly, you could proceed on the assumption that he was much too cunning to wait till the early-morning battle-lines were officially drawn on both sides before making his move: that would have made for a fair fight and Hook avoided fair fights as obsessively as a superstitious person avoids stepping on cracks in the pavement. On the other hand, it would be a bad mistake simply to guess that he would endeavour to surprise you by sallying forth at the crack of dawn, because that is exactly what somebody like Hook would want you to believe. Your next idea, then, might be that he would strike, after all, in the manner and at the time laid down by the Geneva Convention, but Hook would know that you had had that idea and of course act quite differently. He was so dastardly you could not even put it past him to hold back right until tea-time, when you had almost given up hope of there being a battle at all and were starting to pack away your weaponry. Undoubtedly the wisest thing was to prepare for all possible eventualities.

So Peter had guards posted at the ship's port-holes throughout the night, and he himself would swim around every hour on the hour in order to wake them up again. Furthermore he had a fleet of trained carrier dolphins about a league away in each direction, poised to bring news of troop movements in the enemy camp. There was now nothing further to do but wait, the most agonising of all human activities.

The dawn came, delivering rays of fresh sunlight like morning milk on the sea's bottle-green doorstep. On the principle that it's the early fish that catches the worm the myriad inhabitants of the Indian Ocean were already up and conducting their business. By 8 o'clock all the main

marine boulevards around the schooner were a-bustle
with fish swimming to and fro, alone or in formation,
now whimsically curling and drifting like leaves in the
autumn wind, now abruptly changing direction as
though at the command of some invisible tamer with a
whip.

Many of them, passing the ship, were in the habit of
taking a peep through its port-holes as there was always
lots of fun to be had watching the frolics of the
Brotherhood. But today everything appeared strange
and somehow *wrong*. Not one of the only children was
stirring, not even those assigned to the night watch – and
this was because Peter himself had surrendered in the
end to "the honey-heavy dew of slumber", as the Bard
says. Like all children of his age, no matter how
prodigious, and *that* he was, Peter needed at least ten
hours of sleep every night to feel up to the mark next
day; and what with the worrying and the planning and
the counter-planning and the waking up of his less
vigilant fellows he had eventually nodded off in the small
hours of the morn. Even the dolphins, squealing ever
more frantically, were unable to rouse their master.
Ironically, it was not fierce Hook but sleep, gentle
sleep, that had taken Peter unawares and overcome
him.

But why are the dolphins squealing? Because the
enemy is on the march. So very confident is Hook of
victory in the approaching encounter he has chosen the
most unexpected option of all. Without making the
slightest effort at concealment he and his boys advance
boldly in full view, even trumpeting their presence with
a battle chorus composed by Hook himself, who was

something of a lyric poet *dans ses heures*. The tune he set
it to was suspiciously similar to the 'Eton Boating Song':

> "Crow, crow together
> Vic-tor-iously!
> We care not whether
> We bully on land or sea!
>
> For we pick on the littl'uns
> And never fight boys our own size.
> Yes, we pick on the littl'uns
> And the tiniest tots tyrannise!"

Here, a little in advance, ever the partners-in-crime,
are Tupman and Pincher, to whom the reader has
already been introduced. Here, too, is Mouse Minor,
dishonest in every respect but one, that his narrow
slitlike eyes candidly manifest all the malice of which the
brilliant mind behind them is capable. Then comes
Mouse Major, his elder brother, who should have been
hustled off a hundred times to a reformatory school if
his parents had not dearly paid to hush up each of his
misdemeanours; and Scrout, his forte being the cracking
of boys' heads between his bony knees as if they were
walnuts and his limbs a nutcracker; and Marjoribanks
(pronounced 'Marchbanks', a matter about which he
was frightfully particular), who had sold his housemas-
ter's wife into white slavery in Ethiopia for two gold
sovereigns and a second-hand scimitar, and still considered that he had got the best of the bargain; and
Mullins, whose father, it was said, would have been
appointed Chancellor of the Exchequer had it not been
for that unfortunate scalping incident involving the heir

to the Burgravian throne; and 'Bully' Bulstrode, with his diamond- and ruby-studded knuckle-duster; and many another cad as known and feared in the English Home Counties as Hook's pirate crew had been on the Spanish Main.

Since they had not been such a long time under the sea as the only children they were still clothed in the tatters of their school uniforms, so that you could tell to which they had belonged by the colours of their braid. But although it would be unfair to shame the various institutions by reminding the world of their most infamous pupils, prospective parents might be gratified to learn that there also hung about them the tatters of ineradicable refinement. Mouse Major, for instance, who was especially good at garrotting, would never have dreamt of using any but his own old-school tie for that purpose. Even with material so very unpromising the British public-school system had been triumphantly vindicated.

In their midst was Hook himself, that system's most celebrated fallen angel, its veritable Lucifer, and that he meant this to be a red-letter day in his calendar was indicated by the fact that he sported an anemone over his left ear. This morning Hook was at his most dandiacal and diabolical.

A further irony was to count against Peter. Expecting to find him and the children already on the alert, Hook saw no good reason why he should not approach the ship in the open, perhaps hoping to spook the Brotherhood by a display of superior strength. Hence the utter indifference to any idea of concealment and also the rousing battle song. Let them know what they are up against, was his ploy, and they will fall a-quiver to their knees and leave Pan ready for plucking. But when the schooner finally came into view everything about it struck him as unaccountably hushed and still: everything, that is to say, except for one odd sound which his sharp ears were first to pick up.

"Halt, dogs!" cried he. "Belay that hellish caterwauling!"

The bullies, who trembled before anyone even slightly taller than they were, all at once fell silent and waited for Hook to make known his pleasure.

"What is it that you hear, captain?" Smee anxiously asked.

" 'Tis your ugly voice I hear, Smee," replied a menacing Hook, "and if you don't stow it I'll cut your tongue out and give it you to wipe your specs with!"

Smee, quite literally, held his tongue.

Intently cocking an ear, and the anemone that adorned it, Hook took a spyglass from inside his crocodile-suit and directed it at the ship. Then, because of what he saw and heard, a smile creased his blackish lower lip. 'Ware Hook when he smiles.

"Why now, my hearties," he said, in a tone that was suave and creamy, "this job looks to be even easier than I thought; as easy as stealing sweets from the mouth of a babe."

It was, you see, the squealing of the dolphins that Hook had heard. And the irony was that, although these faithful creatures had striven to warn Peter of the enemy's approach, it was instead that enemy which had been informed – informed that Peter and the only children had, on this morning of all mornings, overslept!

"I feel almost sorry for Pan, that I do," sighed Hook, before giving the order to close in. There was a streak of sentimentality in this man as elusive yet as worth waiting for as the green ray which the setting sun is said to emit before it dips over the horizon.

That streak reappeared soon after when he and his bullies had swum silently into the schooner (for, realising that the tactic of surprise would work after all, Hook had immediately abandoned the undeceitful approach: he was not *that* sentimental) and discovered the only children splayed out across their hammocks as haphazardly as if they had been cast there like dice.

For the image of puppies in a basket which had occurred to me when I earlier described the sleeping boys now insinuated itself (quite independently, I assure you) into Hook's diseased brain. Contemplating them, he was momentarily haunted by the thought that he had never had such dear friends in his own childhood, friends with whom he could curl up and feel happy and warm and secure. Even as a cherub-faced infant the only emotions he had ever been capable of inspiring in his fellows were loathing and stark terror. O why should he alone have been—

"An end to these white-livered whimsies!" he muttered, half to himself, half to the deity that had singled him out for such a unique destiny. "To your places, lads, and quietly does it!"

Hook's men quickly dispatched themselves about the ship, taking up positions in ones and twos beside the children, like those butlers who stand pompously behind each of the guests at the Lord Mayor's Banquet. Accompanied by Smee and Scrout, Hook himself made straight for Peter, who lay crumpled up from fatigue with his feet resting between the wooden rungs of the ship's wheel.

All traces of human weakness gone now, he made ready to give the command for each child to be pounced upon at the same time. Just at that instant, however, Peter opened his eyes and, still three-quarters asleep, innocently blinked up at the trio of malevolent faces looming above him.

That look, the lovely, yawny expression of a child one-quarter out of slumber and three-quarters in, it could have affected Hook in two ways. He could even then have taken pity on his helpless prey and held himself back from his most ferocious appetites. Or he could have luxuriously yielded to them.

A coin is tossed inside Hook's mind. Heads he would be cruel, tails he would be kind. The coin pirouettes and pirouettes in ever-depressing circles, till, like a fish thrashing on the bottom of a rowing-boat, it evens itself out on one of its two sides.

Heads it is. (Was he using his double-headed moidore? Nobody will ever know.)

The time for reflection had gone and the time for action had come.

First describing a perfect arc through the ocean, Hook's hook tore savagely at Peter's breast. The boy screamed. Blood oozed out of his body like rats fleeing from a sinking ship. Then he fainted.

Now that it had finally come to this Hook was startled at his own temerity. Peter was his. The moment he had so intensely longed for, longed for for longer than he could remember, that moment had actually

"He clutched at his own throat with his hook."

arrived; but, for the moment, he scarcely knew what to do with his prize. On the one hand he was experiencing that old familiar sense of anti-climax; on the other he felt real incredulity at the idea that he had at last performed the deed he had so often and so lovingly rehearsed. Of one fact was he certain: when his besting of Peter had taken its place on the cloud-capp'd pinnacle of legend, as it soon must do, the boos he would receive would not at all be of the play-acting sort. Which, to a cut-throat of his standing in the community, was of course deeply gratifying, and yet . . .

"Will I give 'im the coop de grace, cap'n?" said Scrout, who was already twitchily fingering a magnificent new penknife. It had a spike for removing stones from horses' shoes that also came in handy for the stabbing of little boys.

"Nay, blast your eyes!" screeched Hook, who seemed horrified at the mere proposal. He turned to his bos'n.

"O Smee, Smee . . . What have I done?"

"Captain?" was all Smee replied, for he felt sure he had not heard the question properly.

But that gave Hook pause, for the last time, to collect himself. He must play out his predestined role to the end, no matter that its taste seemed to have turned strangely bitter in the playing.

"Smee, let's leave these snot-brained noodles to their infantile games. Come," he cried, cordially slipping his hook in the bos'n's arm, "let you and me withdraw from here and return to the cave with Pan. And quickly, too, for we must patch him up or there won't be a drop of life's-blood left in him."

"Why, captain, I had no idea . . ." said Smee, his spectacles misting over with emotion. "True, the boy can still be saved if we go to't soon enough."

"Fool!" snarled Hook, though not as harshly as was his wont. "The only thing I hope to save him from is too swift a death! Now that I have him, I mean to play with him, and I shan't have him a-dying on me till I hear even that boy cry out for his mother!"

"Aye aye, captain," said Smee, half-saddened and half-relieved at the thought that his master's spirits were completely recovered.

So, leaving the bullies to their raucous pleasures, the noise of which could be heard all around them, Hook and Smee carried off Peter to the cave.

There, while Smee laid him out, Hook gloatingly sharpened his hook against a cutlass with the cool professionalism of a butcher honing a pair of carving-knives.

"Draw off the boy's smock," he roared over his shoulder at the bos'n, "to plug up the wound with. Then we'll bring him round, and if we contrive to be subtle in our tormenting of him, why, there'll be pretty entertainment in it for us both!"

Smee – affable, kindly, treacherous Smee – heaved a deep sigh but did as he was told. Naked and vulnerable, Peter was now utterly at the mercy of his arch-enemy.

"Well, now, my indomitable little foe –" purred Hook, feasting bloodshot eyes on his victim.

Whereupon a rather extraordinary thing occurred. At the sight of Peter's glistening body he clutched at his own throat with his hook, gave out a strangulated cry and staggered back in horror. To Smee's amazement Hook's blood had drained so fast from his sallow features that they were now as green as the sea itself.

CHAPTER XII

The Awful Truth

Now, in the chapter just ended, I became so interested in what was happening to Peter at the hands (or rather, the hand) of Hook that I quite forgot to let you know how the other children had fared. If you remember, we left them menaced by Hook's men, who were only waiting for the signal to attack. Well, that signal, when it came, was not issued by Hook himself but, unwittingly, by Peter: when he let out his scream, the bullies, realising that the children would be alerted to the danger, decided to set to at once. With a sense of timing so concerted and exact you might have supposed Hook *had* given a signal they first clasped their hands over their victims' mouths much the way you put a silencer on a revolver. The children squirmed and struggled, but to no avail; even as they attempted to free themselves from their aggressors many of them were buoyed up by the certainty that Peter would, from one moment to the next, swoop down ecstatically to deliver them, but that illusion too, as we know, was a vain one. Ralph put up the fiercest resistance, and managed to black 'Bully' Bulstrode's eye with his own knuckle-duster; but it was three against one and he was soon overwhelmed.

Then, as Hook appeared to have deserted them, the bullies gleefully set about their business without a qualm; and those of you who are in any way squeamish about scenes of violence may wish to skip the following paragraph.

They opened up their whole bag of dirty tricks. As a special treat for having blacked his eye, Bulstrode obliged Ralph to swallow a not very appetising pudding of ice-cream and jelly-fish. Second Helping, still recovering from the last attack, was strung up by Mullins from the stateroom rafters, and he would have had the ship's anchor attached to his neck as extra ballast if Mullins had been able to lift it. Tom-Tom was tarred from his head to his toes, then given a second coating for good measure. Bubbles was swaddled in his own hammock and sent spinning round and round as dizzily as a skipping-rope. Bee had the soles of her feet tickled by the two fraternal Mice, Minor and Major, so that she laughed until she was sick, although it was really no laughing matter. And Miranda, who tried to come to her assistance by shattering the Louis Quinze over Mouse Minor's head, was cornered by Mouse Major, who proceeded to drop sea-spiders down her blouse.

All the children suffered similar indignities. Even Mortimer, who had placidly been minding his own fishy business, was all of a sudden thrust from his goldfish bowl by Marjoribanks. (He may have gasped for a moment or two just for appearances' sake and also in case any of the children were looking on, but he eventually sneaked back into the bowl, proving that he had stayed there all along because he preferred it that way.) When the bullies finally left the ship about an hour later, and the children extricated one another from the various plights in which they found themselves, it was a very bedraggled and bruised Brotherhood that met to have a pow-wow.

In the absence of Peter, Ralph of course became their leader, so it was he who spoke first.

"Look here, boys and girls," he began, "we have just suffered a dreadful defeat, and you all know why, don't you?"

"Because we lost?" proposed Tom-Tom.

Ralph ignored the redundancy. "Because we fell asleep, that's why. In the British Army we would have been court-martialled for falling asleep at our posts."

"If you please, Ralph," ventured one of the smaller ones in a mournful voice, "I don't want to be court-martialled."

"I want to go home," wailed another.

"You are home," protested Ralph.

"No, no!" the children screamed in horror. "This isn't home. There is a place called home, and this isn't it." And even if they all came from different homes, they somehow knew in their hearts that they were speaking of one and the same place.

"I want my mummy," somebody else cried.

"Me too!"

"So do I!"

Not one of the ungrateful little beasts cried out that it was Peter he wanted.

Ralph was a boy as steadfast and true as you might anywhere meet but as a public speaker, unlike Peter, he quite lacked the popular touch, and no phrases came to him that could convince his listeners. It was then that Miranda took the floor, as it were.

"Listen to me, children," she said, "I would like to tell you a story. Once upon a time there was a little girl who lived (on dry land) with her mother and father. Now she loved that mother and father very, very dearly, but she loved them in the way a pup loves its master. It was a respectful, looking-up kind of love. But she had another kind of love to give: the love a pup has for another pup in the same litter, and she was quite often unhappy because she had neither brother nor sister to give that love to. Then one night she heard a call from the depths of the sea and when she answered it she discovered that she had lots of brothers – and even a sister," she added, glancing doubtfully at Bee. "So that became her home, and a very real home it was."

"And did she live happy ever after?" asked Tom-Tom.

"Most of the time," said Miranda cautiously; "but when she was unhappy, you see, she had her brothers and sister to console her."

For a while the children were rather pensive, as they took in Miranda's story. Those among them who understood what she meant by telling it to them enjoyed it because it reminded them of all the good times they had had together, while those who did not understand enjoyed it because it helped them forget the bad times.

"Miranda is right," said Ralph finally. "We ought to remember our oath to the Brotherhood and the rules that Peter taught us."

"But where *is* Peter?" demanded Bubbles. "He ain't skeered of them bullies and lit out?"

"You know that Peter would never betray us."

Ralph spoke with lead in his heart, not because he

believed for a moment that Peter had taken fright and abandoned them but because the word 'betray' grazed his memory's rawest nerve.

"Maybe he has been kidnapped," suggested Bee.

"Why, yes, I'm certain I heard a scream –" Miranda excitedly broke in, "just before I was attacked. I can't say whether it was Peter or not for I've never heard him scream before. Though it did sound like the scream of someone who had never screamed before . . ."

"Then it must be true," cried Ralph. "Peter has been captured by Hook and carried off. It's up to us to rescue him!"

And these children who had perhaps not behaved very well when they needed help shone out now at the idea that they were about to help another. In life the people who do us the most good, as the philosophers know, are not those who help us most but those who most need *our* help.

"We must swim out to Hook's lair," Ralph went on, his cheeks now ablaze with the lust of battle, "rescue Peter and satisfy our honour!"

But, just then, a familiar voice rang out from behind him.

"No!"

It was Peter.

It was Peter all right, though not the Peter they knew. As he swam towards them, they could see instantly that something important had changed in him. His had not been the crude strength of an iron bar but that more subtle strength of an almost invisible wire which, when pressure is exerted upon it, proves to be unbreakable. Yet at last something had come to break the wire: in a way, only his voice was still unbroken. Even the littlest ones felt at once that they were in the presence of a tragedy. For the first time the ocean seemed to them a cold place, and some of them shivered.

Only Miranda, who was not necessarily kinder than the rest but was more matter-of-fact, swam forward to greet him, for she had immediately spied the gash in his breast.

"Why, Peter," she cried, when she remarked how broad and deep the cut was, "you are hurt!"

He turned frowningly away when she tried to touch him. It was clear he had been wounded inside as well as out.

"It's nothing," was all he would say.

"But, Peter, you're bleeding!"

"I tell you it's nothing. It doesn't hurt a bit."

"But where have you been?" she asked. "How worried we all were!"

"If you must know, I was taken by Hook, and this done to me," he replied, carelessly showing his wound. "But I – I escaped."

Now Miranda looked closely at his eyes, which were red-rimmed and puffy.

"Peter," she said in a softer tone, "you've been crying."

"Peter Pan never cries!" he retorted with a flash of his old pride. "I must have something in my eye."

"Have no fear, Peter," said Ralph, after an embarrassed pause had elapsed; "we are ready to avenge you. We shall swim out to Hook's lair and—"

"No!" cried Peter once more.

"But we must repay Hook for the wrong he has done

us all! Do I not speak true?" asked Ralph, this time meaningfully addressing his question to the children rather than to Peter.

Before they could answer, Peter spoke again.

"There's nothing to be done about it. Hook and his bullies were too strong for us." He winced as if he could hardly believe what he himself was saying. "We've been beaten, and now we ought to be good sports. We must go away, all of us, and make our home somewhere else. There are other fish in the sea, other ships, other seas. Oh, I do so want to leave this beastly place and go as far away as possible and never see it again!" he howled with a fierceness that startled his audience and sent shudders through his own battered little body.

"Go away?" said Ralph unbelievingly. "Run away?"

Miranda interrupted. "I'm certain Peter doesn't mean we should run away. Not *run* away – that's not what you meant, Peter, was it?"

"Yes, oh yes!" Peter cried bitterly, realising that he would have to drink the poisoned cup to the very last drop. "Yes, I mean that we should run away. It's too dangerous for us to stay."

"You are afraid, Peter Pan," said Ralph, looking directly into his eyes.

There was a time when Peter might have knocked Ralph down for that or had him banished from Wet Land or just laughed merrily in his face and retaliated that he did not know the meaning of the word 'afraid'. And there was a time when that would actually have been true. Now it was obvious that the meaning of the word knew him. Sometimes it is words that look *us* up.

"We waste time," he said flatly. "We must make ready for the journey."

The children knew no longer what to believe or whom to obey. They looked anxiously from Peter's face to Ralph's and back again, while the two boys stared each other down.

It was Ralph who spoke first, with a strange glow all at once seeming to enhalo him.

"I will not be with thee, Peter. Nay, even if I alone have to beard Hook in his den, I will not leave unavenged such a mean, cowardly attack."

Being a boy of very few words as a rule, Ralph was surprised at having spoken so much in the past quarter-of-an-hour and more particularly at having had the effrontery to stand up to Peter. However, in that last little declaration of his, he had employed two words which, just in themselves, would turn out to represent a momentous watershed in the politics of Wet Land. What could they have been? 'Nay' and 'thee' – that was all he needed to win the children over to his cause. For, as I told you, it was just the kind of language that Peter would instinctively fall into when about to embark upon a great adventure; it was the language of a born leader – and here was Ralph using it with consummate ease while Peter's own language had been depressingly dull and business-like.

Slowly to begin with, allowing themselves to drift instead of actively swimming, as if it were the mere current of the ocean and not that of any transference of loyalty that swayed their decision, they edged closer and closer to Ralph and further and further away from Peter. A few of them attempted in vain to resist the current.

They appeared still to be waiting for Peter to cast off this lethargy that had settled on him and assert himself in the old manner. Even those who had already aligned themselves with the new order and were now shoulder to shoulder with Ralph went on obscurely hoping that it would happen, even Ralph himself secretly wished it so. But it was not to be. For when Peter spoke at last, and what he said was potentially capable of stemming the tide, he made the grave mistake of uttering his words ineffectually, almost regretfully, when of course he ought to have thundered them out as from the bridge of a ship.

"This is, you know, mutiny."

"No," Ralph replied calmly, speaking for all of them. "For mutiny means to disobey one's commander, and that you have ceased to be."

Is this the end of Peter Pan? Is he, even in repartee, to be eclipsed?

With the prospect of scores to be settled, excitement already ran high. The children bustled about, often pointlessly but always pleasurably, assigning or being assigned tasks, hunting up suitable weapons and regaling one another with accounts of just what they intended to do to their respective tormentors. Meanwhile Bee, who was starting to recover some of her natural busybodiness, was pointedly advising them all that, if anybody felt in the least like going somewhere, he or she had better go now, as it would not be possible to stop for that once they were on their way.

Did none of them have a parting word or thought for Peter? I know not exactly why – perhaps it was because, being the newest member of the Brotherhood, her feeling of loyalty was not yet worn away from use; perhaps it was because she had read about Peter Pan and felt that something must be dreadfully wrong for him to behave in such a fashion; or perhaps it is merely that she is the nearest we have to a heroine in this story and it is right that she should make the gesture – but Miranda approached Peter and took his hand in hers.

"Peter," she said softly, "do come with us. It is what we all want you to do."

"No."

"But, Peter—"

"No, I say."

"Do you wish me to think you are afraid?"

"You may think what you please," he answered, as if it were a matter of total indifference to him. "But I am not afraid. To know the meaning of the word 'afraid' and yet not be afraid, perhaps that's what it means to be a truly brave person."

"So you know the meaning of the word 'afraid'?"

"Yes," Peter replied sadly. "I do now."

"Afraid of what exactly?"

"That's my business."

There was a pause before Miranda spoke again.

"Where will you go?"

"I haven't decided yet, but far, far away."

"To escape Hook?"

"Aye. The ocean's not big enough for both of us."

"Then why don't you kill him?"

Peter sharply drew his hand away. "How strange," said he, "to hear a little girl talk so calmly of killing."

She looked intently into Peter's face. Were those lines under his eyes?

Could Peter Pan be growing up?

But that is of course absurd; for children do not really age, they change. So let us simply say that Peter had changed and that, from the look of things, nothing about him would ever be quite the same again.

Miranda was given no time to puzzle out the mystery, however. Ralph had gathered the Brotherhood together for a morale-boosting talk, wherein he mentioned that it was a mission from which some of them would not come back alive, among other comforting details, for which he was cheered lustily. Then off they set, armed to the teeth, and in a few cases armed with little more than their teeth. With one last glance backwards at Peter, who was still defiant but looked so terribly forlorn by himself, Miranda tightly clasped the hairbrush with which she meant to give Mouse Major a taste of his own unpleasant medicine and joined the other children.

Through the sea moss and lichen they advanced, swimming close to the ocean floor in order to avoid being detected and making no louder sound as they glided than fingers make when rippling across the strings of a harp. Though they had only a very vague notion of where Hook's hideout might be situated, in fact finding it proved much less troublesome than they imagined. For after the morning's excesses the bullies were indulging themselves in a bacchanalian orgy of gin, dice and cards, and their strident laughter and vulgar cursing could be heard a mile around. It was perplexing that Hook, that master tactician, would permit his dogs to give away their position in so foolhardy a manner, but for the moment the most pressing concern of the children was to approach the cave without being spotted first.

Suddenly, as he surged up over the top of a long coral ridge, Ralph signalled for them all to halt and pointed in silence to the valley that lay beneath them. There it was, Hook's cave! He could already make out the entrance, near which the bullies lay sprawled about with gin bottles in their laps and, on their faces, expressions of indescribable degeneracy. And there too, a little apart, were Hook and Smee.

Even from afar it was evident that the sharp little red night-lights in Hook's eyes had been extinguished. His greasy tresses drooped low and uncurled over his brow as if made out of candle-wax. It could have been an optical illusion produced by the ocean sway, but Ralph was prepared to swear that his hook was also drooping. Not even Barbecue's cabin boy, still wet behind the ears, would have been afraid of him at this moment.

At a sign from Ralph the children began their descent, making themselves as tiny and compact and inconspicuous as minnows. Nary a murmur passed between them nor any uncalled-for gesture to ruffle the green silence of the sea: 'twas almost as if they were gently sliding down the current and straight into Hook's encampment. And it was only when Tupman, momentarily aroused from his drunken torpor, blinked up at them with eyes so transfixed his monocle dropped out that Ralph gave the signal to attack.

"Down, boys and girls, down and at them!"

Needing no further encouragement they swooped on the bullies like a flock of birds.

Had the latter been in a fighting-fit state it is certain that they would have won easily: they were taller and stronger and had far more English bully beef sticking to

their bones. But drunk as they were, sated with debauchery, without the Captain to egg them on with his hook, and having to spend most of the battle warding off blows with their hands, they found no opportunity to move into the offensive. Second Helping pummelled Tupman and Pincher so hard that the two youths, like the snivelling cry-babies all bullies are underneath, were soon tearfully begging for mercy. Miranda sought out Mouse Major and began to hammer him with her hairbrush into the soft, shifting sand, like a nail into wet plaster, till only his head was visible. Bubbles quietly and methodically set to shovelling the overflow of that sand into Mullins' mouth, not troubling to remove any of the creepy-crawly insects that inhabited it (the sand, I

"He skipped up and down the shingle, playing
gaily on his heartless pipes."

mean). As for Bee, she quite simply, and without making any fuss about it, scalped everyone within reach. Revenge, they discovered, *was* sweet.

And Hook? It seemed that nothing at first could shake him out of the apathetic state into which he had declined. Then gradually, as though he had just noticed that Peter was not among the children, his eyes started to glow a pale watery rose colour and became redder and redder and narrower and narrower until at last they were two crimson cracks of fury. He pulled himself up to his full height and surveyed the carnage around him.

" 'S'death! 'S'blood! And split me infinitives! What be this?" he cried out to what remained of his men. "Is't of these babes-in-arms that you be affrighted? If you aren't on top o' them in ten seconds flat, by thunder I'll have Johnny Hook here skewer you all at once and make meself a bully kebab!"

It was merely a threat, and with more than a hint of Hookian hyperbole about it, yet it was enough to turn the tide of battle. There was no order of Hook's that the bullies would not obey, even if it meant overcoming their natural cowardliness. One by one they started to fight back, with tooth and nail and any other handy part of the body. The Captain himself, taking the enemy's measure, ascertained that it was Mouse Minor who had tackled Ralph; and he casually jerked him to one side with his hook, that he might come face to face with the boy.

"So you are henceforth the leader of this rag-tag-and-bobtail crew, are you?" he snarled. "Then prepare to meet your maker; but first you'll have to meet your breaker, James Aloysius Hook, Esq., at your service."

Ralph quailed at the sight of his adversary, but he was a lad of no mean courage, and he silently prayed that that courage would not leave him now. Indeed it was of greater use to him than his knife, for he lacked the very rudiments of cut-and-thrust duelling and could only pretend to lunge and parry as he had seen Peter do. It was, then, hardly to be wondered at that Hook gained the upper-hand at once; and so confident was he about the outcome he could afford to draw back every so often and insolently manicure a nail with the tip of his hook before striking at Ralph again with cat-like cunning.

But it was not long before the cut-throat began to grow blasé with his play-acting and decided to bring both it and Ralph's life to a speedy conclusion. With a single dazzling feint, one he could have made at almost any stage of their duel, he knocked the knife out of the boy's grasp and stood poised to sink the hook into his breast. Fortunately, however, at that precise moment he chanced to raise his eyes heavenwards, and what he saw caused him suddenly to cower back in fear, or in shame.

Ralph, you may imagine, seized the occasion thus granted him by his assailant's unexpected disarray. Quickly recovering his knife, he was about to plunge it into Hook when once more a commanding voice rang out.

"Stop!" it cried with all its boyish might. "O stop! Do not kill that man!"

Ralph turned. It was Peter, perched yet again on that same coral rock.

"But why, Peter, why?" asked Ralph; yet at the very

instant he posed the question he already knew what its answer must be.

"Because," said Peter, gritting his little milk-teeth, *"he is my father."*

CHAPTER XIII

The Adventure Ends

*N*o boy is an island, not even Peter Pan.

He who prided himself that he was free as the air, without roots or branches, he who lived on an island and flew through the sky and dived to the bottom of the sea, in order to unshackle himself from the ties to which the rest of humankind is bound, not even he was able to escape his destiny in the end. And if the destiny of a grown-up lies ahead in the future, that of a child must be sought out in the past – a past that stretches back to the time before he was born. Peter had a past, too; and although he had struggled hard to cast it off as he did his shadow, it was more securely attached to him than any shadow and would follow him around always.

Yes, Peter was Hook's own little son. But since the origin of their quarrel has been lost in the clouds of time, since Peter could scarcely remember ever having had a father and Hook had never told any of his men, not even Smee, that he had ever had a son, we can only conjecture how it all came about.

For instance, we know from hints dropped by Peter to the children in their last hours together that what made Hook recoil in such anguish from Peter's naked body was the sight of an unusually shaped birthmark on his left thigh. In deference to a certain aristocratic British family I am honour-bound not to reveal the exact nature of that birthmark, but I can say that it is to be found exclusively on the thighs of one noble lineage, 'handed down' from generation to generation, so to speak, like an heirloom, and changing from the right thigh to the left as son succeeds father: Hook's therefore was on the right. I can also state that when the Captain thus discovered his kinship with Peter he had tried to embrace the boy and, when he was scornfully rebuffed, had broken down and sobbed bitterly; and even if he was dressed in a crocodile-suit they were not at all crocodile tears that he shed. I shall further venture to say that what Hook could be heard moaning, over and over again, was "Oh, Mary, Mary . . .", and in that instant Peter recalled how for him the name 'Mary', although long expunged from his memory, had once been a word with the same meaning – a synonym, as we call it – as 'mother'. But what fearful wrong Hook might once have done his wife Mary, and whether Peter had witnessed that wrong-doing, and how he had subsequently come to be on the Neverland alone, none of us will ever know for sure. Perhaps if you or I had Captain James Hook for a father, we too would not have wanted to grow up. These are deep waters, as deep as any in the Indian Ocean.

That was Peter's story and his destiny. And though, when last we saw them, Hook in his shame and confusion appeared almost to be urging Ralph on to strike him down, the boy stayed his blow. As for Smee, it would be fair to say that he was simply flabbergasted, and even the bullies looked humbled. There was a split second when absolutely nothing happened, when time was suspended, when all of them, Peter and Hook and Smee, children and bullies alike, presented a picture of arrested movement recalling the wax figures at Madame Tussaud's.

Then of all the unexpected things you could ever imagine occurring the most truly unexpected thing did occur.

'Old Faithful' erupted.

It began with a faint rumbling noise in the distance, causing all heads to turn at the same time. Could it, was the thought that went through each of those heads, could it be hammock-time already? No, it wasn't possible, they had been wakened from sleep so rudely only such a short while before. Yet the rumbling grew louder and louder – much louder, indeed, than they had ever heard the volcano rumble – and there was a panicky, trapped quality to the sound like that made by boiling water in a saucepan when it seethes underneath the lid. As though by instinct, the children hurried to put their hands over their ears. Just in time, too, for a moment later they heard a loud explosion, which made the sea gradually turn a lurid maroon colour and become as warm and foamy as bath-water; and when they believed that really nothing else could happen, the floor suddenly began to heave and shake beneath them, and lots of strange gassy bubbles spurted out of the sand.

Peter, like a born leader, rallied his flock.

"Quick!" he shouted, reassuring them at once that the real Peter Pan was back. "It's an earthquake! Link hands, all of you, each take the other's hand and don't forget the little ones!"

"But where can we go?" asked Ralph, who was once more a born second-in-command.

"Up!" cried Peter. "Up, up to the surface!"

He straightway seized Miranda's hand, ordered her to seize Tom-Tom's, then Tom-Tom to grab a hold of Second Helping's, and so forth. As fast as they could plough through the water, the little human daisy-chain started to rise to the surface.

However their first impression, when they peered down beneath them, was that they weren't rising at all, and it took a minute or so for them to realise that the ocean floor was rising with them! Creaking and lurching, as if the centre of the earth had at last been disgorged from its immemorial resting-place, it resembled a sinking ship in reverse, and shoals of fish, small and large, all of them belonging to different clans, if you like, so all of them wearing different tartans, darted hither and thither to escape its inexorable advance.

The bullies in their inebriated condition were caught up by the onrush; and as the volcanic eruption was already taking the pyramidal shape more or less of a mountain, they found themselves being rolled this way and that up and down its slopes, desperately latching on to a plant, a rock, a bit of reef, anything that might slow down their dizzying whirl through the maëlstrom. The children last and furthest down on the chain, too, felt their toes starting to touch the rising ground and they were soon tumbling on to it in a heap. One behind the next, right up to Peter himself, they folded up on top of each other in the manner of an accordion; so that when, with a terrific cascade of spray, the mountain burst through the surface of the ocean, they were lying helter-skelter all over the place, their little hearts beating frantically in time.

Even on the surface the mountain continued to rise. Of course it was the topmost tip that nosed itself out first, a tip on which Peter was precariously perched. Then more and more of it appeared, it spread about in every direction and acquired slopes both gentle and precipitous and foothills and a beach where the sandy areas had been and a dense entanglement of vegetation and a lagoon where a large hollow in the ground had managed to trap the scooped-up sea-water, and the schooner which had once served as the only children's home lay as though wrecked on the beach and crabs began to crawl out of the sands and serpents to slither through the vegetation and there were just enough fish in the lagoon to propagate every conceivable species of fish and in no time at all exotically plumed macaws and cockatoos were circling the spot in search of comfortable nooks in which to build their nests and rear their young. Soon redskins and mermaids and pirates would be haunting this island as of old.

It was, in short, the Neverland.

As yet, however, let it be merely a new uncharted island in the ocean, an island on which the only children had been shipwrecked – but from underneath. Like shipwrecked sailors they puffed and panted, and those who were semi-conscious were just about able to murmur "Where am I?" in the dazed tones of a lady coming to after a fainting fit. Some of them had almost forgotten how to inhale and exhale properly: for a few seconds they choked and gulped, beating their heels against the sand like fish out of water. But not for much longer than a few seconds: very quickly they were breathing in the fresh air as greedily as though it were raspberry jam.

And while I am speaking of fish, I ought to mention perhaps that Mortimer's bowl, having handily lodged itself during the earthquake in a crater that was just the right size for it, was also carried up to the surface. There it stood, incongruously, on the shore, its one occupant still amiably doing the rounds, his gills slightly ruffled after the tremendous shock to his system.

But now we are coming to the very end of our story. And since I am not at all fond of prolonged leave-takings I shall try to recount the final scenes of the adventure as swiftly as they took place.

So many things seemed to occur all at once. No sooner had our children gathered themselves up and rejoiced to find that they were all safe and sound, not a single one missing, than they were startled to hear the loud and insistent tooting of a ship's horn. There, lying at anchor not too far away offshore, was a fine white steamer exactly like the one from which Miranda had been abducted. Well, to be honest, if you were to have inspected it more closely and critically, you would have said that it was smaller and possibly a trifle less grand, but what made the resemblance was the fact that standing together on the deck and gazing raptly over the side were two former acquaintances of ours whom you have doubtless quite forgotten in the meantime: I refer to Major Porter and his darling Lillibet!

And just in case you find such an opportune arrival beginning to strain your credulity, that credulity which has been so patient and indulgent up till now, I should point out that their presence in the region was by no means the coincidence it might appear.

It so happened that the very last words addressed to her by her fellow-passenger, the noted Scottish author, had made a deep impression on Mrs. Porter, so deep she found them difficult to shake from her mind. "It would be a tragedy, Mrs. Porter, a dreadful, needless tragedy if you were to mistake such a play-death for the real thing!" What on earth had he meant by that? she could not help wondering. What if, after all, he had spoken true? What if Miranda's death, that had certainly appeared as conclusive and mortal as any death could be, were mere play-acting?

Resolved not to rest until she had uncovered the truth, Mrs. Porter had inserted an advertisement in the Personal Column of *The Times*, inviting the parents of all the other only children who had so mysteriously disappeared to come forward; and so great was the sincerity and the passion that could be read into her beautiful eyes when she spoke to them of her hopes, every one agreed to join her in the search. Thus, not long afterwards, they chartered a steamer, had it rigged out for a lengthy voyage, set full speed ahead for the Indian Ocean, and there we are.

(By the by, do you remember the strong, manly chin I lent the Major that he might bear up the more valiantly during the troubled times that lay ahead of him? Well, now that his ordeal was drawing to its close, I naturally thought I could remove it again without causing him too much distress, and what do you suppose I found? A real chin just as strong and manly as the one I had lent him. Tested in the crucible of adversity, you see, the Major had begun to acquire a new inner strength that could not but be reflected in his outward aspect, and he had no further need of any assistance of mine.)

Back on the island – while Hook's bullies all sat skulking in a huddle, watched over by the ever-benign Smee, and Hook himself was nowhere to be seen – the children were preparing joyfully, and perhaps a little sadly as well, to leave. If not one of them asked Peter for permission to go, it was because they had emerged from the depths of the ocean as though from the depths of sleep, and in the clear, bright light of day Peter struck them as just another little boy like themselves from whom it would feel rather foolish to be receiving orders. As children do, they all somehow understood that this particular chapter in their story was well and truly over; as at the end of a pantomime, when, with your right arm already confusingly inside the left sleeve of your over-coat and your left arm half inside the right sleeve, you take one last fond look at the stage on which so many wonderful adventures have been enacted, they had the impression that a red-and-gold curtain had descended to separate them for ever from their erstwhile leader.

And if Miranda, clutching Mortimer's bowl (for which she had already picked out a nice sunny position atop the drawing-room mantelpiece at home), did try to persuade Peter to return with her, it was with the awful foreknowledge that, as she had once read in a book, another little girl had failed to do just that.

He was standing quite alone on the beach.

"Get your things, Peter," she cried, shaking.

"No," he answered, pretending indifference, "I am not going with you, Miranda."

"Yes, Peter."

"No."

To show that her departure would leave him un-
moved, he skipped up and down the shingle, playing
gaily on his heartless pipes. She had to run about after
him, though it was rather undignified.

"To find your mother," she coaxed.

"No, no," he told Miranda decisively; "perhaps she
would say I was old, and I just want always to be a little
boy and to have fun. Besides, I still have a score to settle
with Hook, and I will finish him off yet, or my name's
not Peter Pan!"

Had he forgotten that Hook was his father? Probably.

Miranda made one last attempt.

"But, Peter—"

"No."

And so the others had to be told.

"Peter isn't coming."

Peter not coming! Alas, I have to say that this time
nothing seemed feigned about the indifference with
which the only children greeted Miranda's news. They
had eyes only for the two small boats which even now
were approaching the island to carry them away from it
for good. For all I know, they had as thoroughly
forgotten that Peter had once been their leader and
friend as Peter himself had forgotten he was his arch-
enemy's son.

There was one more surprise in store for them all.

Of course they boarded the ship to be reunited with
their mothers and fathers (while the bullies were put in
the hold). And of course, as you expect of such re-
unions, lots of tears were mixed up together with smiles –

which is the best and deepest form of emotion you can ever feel – as well as a few scolding words, but these were not very severe: since parents make children what they are, what then is the use of scolding them? The big surprise awaiting them, however, was their discovery that, with a single exception, each of them in their absence had been given either a baby brother or sister (and, in the case of Second Helping, both) so that none of them could any longer be thought of as 'only'.

Were they pleased? Yes, naturally, they were quite delighted. No signs of jealousy? Oh well, perhaps just a few.

The exception I mentioned was Miranda herself, who looked dreadfully crestfallen at being singled out so. But it takes time, as she would learn, to bring a baby brother or sister into the world, more time than she had actually spent in Wet Land, and I trust I am not betraying any confidence if I reveal that her joy was only postponed, that in a very few months – but there, I have said enough already and I must let Mrs. Porter break the news to her when she is good and ready.

Now, as the ship steams away towards the beckoning horizon, and at its rail they stand, mother, father and child, watching the island recede in the distance, let's eavesdrop on them just one last time before we, too, take our leave.

"Oh look, mother and father," is what we hear Miranda cry out, "can't you see them? It is Peter and Hook!"

For there indeed they were, as clear as day, on the very top of the mountain, duelling as furiously and as happily as if nothing had ever come to interrupt their age-old quarrel.

The Major dutifully cupped his hand over his brow and screwed up his eyes.

"I'm afraid I can't see anything, my child," he answered after a moment; "only sunlight glinting through the tops of trees."

"Can't you either, mother darling?" asked Miranda anxiously.

"Why, yes, Miranda," said Mrs. Porter thoughtfully, "I can see something, certainly, a glow that sparkles on the mountain. But it is all dreadfully blurry, my dear, and it looks more like a fairy, I should say. Could it possibly be," she asked with a smile, "Tinker Bell instead of Peter Pan and Captain Hook?"

Peter and Hook it was nevertheless, though perhaps it is only children who will ever be able to see them clearly, for that glow that the grown-ups see is nothing else but the aura that surrounds all timeless legends.

I have said that the island turned into the Neverland. It may well be, then, that the sequence of events which I have faithfully recorded in this book takes place before rather than after certain other events about which you may have read in another book, or even that all of these events together lie outside of time as we earthbound mortals understand it, and that the return of Peter and Hook to the Neverland is what we would call an Eternal Return, and that they will go on for ever, lunging and parrying, quarrelling and perhaps secretly loving, to the ends of the earth and the end of time. For thus it has always been between fathers and sons, and thus it will always be, so long as grown-ups are stern and sinful and forgiving and children are gay and innocent and heartless.